world out of mind

world out of mind

BY J. T. M'INTOSH

doubleday & company, inc., garden city, new york

library of congress catalog card number 53–6252

copyright, 1953, by james macgregor, all rights reserved
printed in the united states at
the country life press, garden city, n.y.

world out of mind

book one

chapter one

THE SWING DOORS OPENED AND TWO MEN AND A WOMAN came into the foyer. At the far end of a long passage Raigmore moved away from the list of theater shows which he had been scanning and went slowly toward the elevators, not looking up. Out of the corner of his eye he saw the two men sit down by the swing doors and the woman come towards the elevator, toward him.

He looked up at her when it was natural to look at her, and stared frankly because that was natural too. Anything else would have been unnatural. She was twenty-three and obviously somebody. The mere fact that she wore no badge, coming straight off the street, would have been sufficient reason for him to stare at her. Her beauty was another, and the probability that he had recognized her as Alison Hever was a third.

So as they came together, Raigmore ambling casually and Alison walking briskly, she had no reason to notice him specially, despite his obvious interest in her, until it became clear that he was also going up in the elevator. She checked her stride slightly so that she could take the elevator he didn't, for no reason except that White Stars generally avoided even the most fleeting personal contact with strangers who might know or guess that they were White Stars. There was no obstinacy about it; when Raigmore also checked himself and bowed her into the elevator in front of him she smiled pleasantly and stepped inside without hesitation.

Raigmore raised his eyebrows inquiringly as the doors slid shut. "Fourteenth," she said. She had noticed his black badge now. Even in her, the sight of the badge produced caution and a certain distrust. Who could trust a Black?

The caution was understandable. Who *could* trust a Black? Nobody. Not even another Black.

As the elevator moved smoothly upward, Raigmore said abruptly: "I'm Eldin Raigmore. I suggest you remember the name, Alison, because one day you'll marry me."

It was the kind of thing that was only to be expected of a Black. Alison wasn't surprised. She smiled faintly but did nothing and said nothing. Only when she stepped out on the fourteenth floor did she acknowledge Raigmore's existence again.

"I liked the way you said that and nothing more," she admitted. Her manner was easy and pleasant, with only a hint of ironic amusement. "It suggested an understanding of tactics that's lost in a Black. Why not take the Tests, Raigmore?" Her voice, inevitably, became more ironic as she went on: "If you should turn out to be a White Star—why, then, what you said is probably correct."

She walked along the corridor, but at the corner she

paused for a moment and looked back at him over her shoulder, curiously. There was something about the way she did it that showed that curiosity was one of her main characteristics. She was curious about everything, interested in everything. Even Eldin Raigmore.

He knew what she was doing in the hotel. She was going to visit Gloria Clarke, a friend of hers—and, as any friend of a White Star was likely to be, high in the Test ranks. Gloria was a Yellow Star, three grades below Alison—but still in the top one per cent of one per cent of one per cent.

Raigmore went down in the elevator again. That was all he intended to do for the moment. Eldin Raigmore now existed. After all, one didn't have to prove existence. A White Star knew Eldin Raigmore existed, and that, for the moment, was good enough.

Later it would seem strange that no record of Eldin Raigmore existed before two days ago—May 23. That was something which still had to be dealt with, a problem to which a solution had to be found.

He met Fred Salter in the foyer. Like Alison, Salter didn't know him from Adam. In his two days of reconnoitering Raigmore had made sure that no one who mattered or might matter, like Alison or Salter, had had a chance to notice him. Now he was ready. It was time for them to notice him.

He made sure he got in Salter's way so that they had to be conventionally polite, apologizing and stepping aside, and Salter had to look at him.

"Sorry," said Salter. "My fault for not looking where you were going."

Raigmore knew that was meant to be humor, but he wasn't sure enough of what humor actually was to attempt to answer in the same vein. He grinned instead, knowing that was a natural reaction when anyone made a joke, and stepped past Salter.

Salter had seen someone outwardly not unlike himself— a tall man of about twenty-five, dark-haired, blue-eyed. The likeness was not startling and quite fortuitous; still, Salter would remember him.

Salter, presumably, was also going up to see Gloria Clarke, who was either a girl friend or a relative of his. Raigmore didn't know which. If Salter hadn't met Alison Hever before, he would meet her now. Possibly Alison would mention her encounter with Raigmore and they would discuss him. All the better.

Raigmore looked curiously at the two men who waited by the doors. He did it so that they became interested enough to examine him.

They were not exactly a bodyguard, these two. Senseless crime was rare these days. Theft, no—it wasn't senseless to steal when you thought you could get away with it. Shoplifting, safebreaking, car stealing—these things were still done, though they weren't the flourishing professions they had once been, and had to be done much more carefully. But murder was another thing. To have anything to gain from murder you had to have a lot to lose. And these days you were practically certain to lose it.

So these men weren't around to guard Alison against assassins. Except in a police state, assassination is always very easy for a competent killer. They were there because a White Star, and particularly Alison Hever, the only living White Star under forty, often needed protection from her admirers.

Having stared at the men and made them notice him, Raigmore went through the swing doors into the street. His task proper was begun.

When he was well clear of the building, on his way back to the modest hotel at which he was staying, a girl who had been waiting detached herself from a wall and fell into step beside him. Raigmore paid no attention. He had never seen her before.

"No, you don't know me," the girl agreed with his unspoken thought. "I'm supposed to contact you. And take orders from you."

She was a tiny blonde, as beautiful as Alison in a mass-produced sort of way, but without a suggestion of the qualities that made Alison a White Star. She wore the Purple Cross. That was her rating for life. Being a Purple Cross, she could be absolutely free in her manner, her dress, her talk, her attitude to life. She wore a plastic dress over a lopsided slip that was all modesty on the right and immodest to the current limit on the left.

As a Purple Cross she was above the Browns and Blacks and Grays and Purple Circles—above most of the population of the world, in fact—and yet not so high in the Test hierarchy that she had to be careful about what she did, or care much what people thought about her. She was high enough to be proud and free, but not high enough to be fettered again by the natural responsibility of all leaders of men and women.

Raigmore remained silent.

"May 23," said the girl. "Four miles from Millo. A wood. I was there, watching, but I'd been told not to identify myself to you at once. Only to follow you around, get in touch with you when you seemed ready, and do anything you say."

"You did it well," Raigmore remarked. "While I was watching others I never suspected that I was being watched myself."

"You had to find things out. I didn't. I only had to see where you went."

Raigmore decided to accept her on her own valuation. He had known there would be others but that he was the leader. Acceptance didn't mean much. There was no need to tell her anything.

"You will do anything I say," he observed. "With what limitations?"

"None," she replied emotionlessly. "And with no questions."

"Murder?" he asked casually.

"Of course."

"Do you know of any others?"

"Yes. A woman and a man. But they will introduce themselves to you. They don't concern me. I take orders from you, unless you tell me I am to take them from someone else."

It was all very cold and businesslike. And therefore, somehow wrong. Dimly, hazily, Raigmore recognized the missing factor.

"We have been talking," he said evenly, "as if we didn't belong to this planet. Or to this race."

She hesitated, then nodded. "So we have."

"What's your name?"

"Peach Railton."

"Well, Peach, the part you seem to have chosen looks right. From now on, play it. All the time. Even when you're alone with me. Understand?"

She understood. She obeyed. There was a subtle, immediate change in the way she held her body, in the glints in her eyes. She had become what she looked, with the consummate precision of the trained spy of any race—first observing, then imitating.

There was still something missing, but Raigmore couldn't tell her about that. He didn't know about it. It was missing in him too.

He knew a lot, and he was rapidly learning more from books, novels, newspapers and his own observation. He knew all about all the emotions—anything about them that could be written down.

But he had never experienced emotion. So he didn't see, as Alison or Salter might have seen, that while Peach acted her part flawlessly there wasn't a shadow of feeling behind it.

chapter two

THE TESTS WERE TRUSTED. THEY WERE NEARLY PERFECT— most people thought they *were* perfect. But perfection is incapable of improvement, and the Tests were still changing and being improved, if but slightly. Any test of human capacities can be trustworthy only to a little less than the current limit of human capacity, and it was not until many Whites had passed through the Tests, and each produced his thesis on the system, that the top limits of the Test territory began to approach the lower regions in completeness and efficiency.

Fred Salter was still In Test, for he had come to Earth from Mars only fairly recently, and Mars so far had no Test facilities. Raigmore went to the same Tests Depot as Salter, without any concrete plan for making use of the circumstance. He might meet Salter again, but that would be left to chance.

A girl attendant was reading a magazine as he entered. She laid it down and stood up. On the desk in front of her was a little stand with her name on a card—Sally Morris. She didn't ask what he wanted. There was only one thing he could want. She was going to ask "What stage?" but then Raigmore turned so that she could see his black badge.

She looked faintly surprised. She was an intelligent-looking girl. All Test operators had to be intelligent, but most of them were unambitious and patient. She wore a plain white coat, like a doctor. It bore no badge. She had to tell people who were In Test what to do. It might be a little awkward if she was wearing, say, a purple star and ordering about Orange Circles.

"How much do you want to do today?" she asked.

"Just the first Test."

"Very well." She led him to a small booth with a thick,

soundproof door. It contained nothing but a chair and a keyboard with a blank screen behind it.

"Your name is . . . ?"

Raigmore gave it. She didn't ask for his address. Later more details would be wanted, but the first Test didn't call for them.

It was supposed to be impossible to fool the Tests. He could have come in wearing any badge he liked, plus the green, and said he wanted to start at the appropriate stage; but the results would show the fraud.

The girl held out her hand. It took him a second or two to realize what she wanted. Then he reached to his lapel and removed the black badge. He was no longer a Black— no longer Untested. He would never wear the black again.

"When the screen lights up," the girl told him, "you will press any of these buttons, as you wish, one at a time. Your score will show in the screen. Watching it, you will attempt to increase it by operating the buttons. At the end of ten minutes you'll hear a buzzer and the screen will register your final score. That's all."

She gave him a card containing in detail what she had said. Then she turned to the door.

"You have five minutes now to think about this Test," she said. "Then the screen will light up."

She went out quietly and closed the door.

Raigmore had a certain theoretical knowledge of the Tests, that was all. It was confined to what one could read about them in an encyclopedia. There was a lot in the encyclopedia, but nothing that would help anyone to do the Tests better than he would in ignorance.

He considered the first Test. It must be principally an estimate of intelligence. He thought it was likely that he could pass the entire series with high distinction, and he had already decided he must be full out from the beginning. It might surprise the operator that a man who had no previous Test record and was obviously at least twenty-five should make an astonishingly high score in this preliminary Test, but that couldn't be helped. Knowing as little as he did about the Tests, he could not afford to try to double-cross them, doing well but not too well.

Sooner or later as he proceeded with the Tests the authorities would want to know about his past record, as he climbed higher and higher. He would have to do something very soon to build up some sort of history behind him. The fact that his life had begun on May 23 was inadmissible.

Presumably Peach Railton had also had a short history, though not quite as short as his. But it didn't matter much that the previous history of a Purple Cross was shrouded in mystery. A Purple Cross didn't have such talent that her past must be outstanding or even very interesting.

Raigmore's trump card was the way the Tests were trusted. On that his whole strategy rested. If it were a question of believing the Tests or almost anything else, the Tests were to be believed.

But the screen had lit up, and now all that concerned him was how to perform his Test.

Before him was a block of buttons arranged in a square, fifteen to a side—225 of them. He pressed the button at the bottom right-hand corner, knowing a system must emerge. The screen showed the figure 10. He touched the button immediately above, and the figure changed to 9. The button above that dropped the score to 8.

Pressing buttons at random would obviously result in a low score. The purpose was to find a system. Any system was better than none, despite the screen's warnings. He touched the fourth button in the row. The screen showed 11.

Rapidly he repeated the series from that point. The score dropped twice and then jumped three, as before. He could plod on with the same system, and no doubt many people did.

But the challenge of the Tests was that they were no easier the second time. That must mean that each Test was unique, and that instruction by someone who had taken the Test would not help. The pauses must be measured, and there must be something measuring mental effort, so that if anyone tried to perform the Test by rote it would immediately be obvious. The light seemed normal, but perhaps encephalographic patterns were being computed as he sat there.

He tried various series. He discovered rapidly that the more complicated a series the higher it scored. At the same time, a simple series continued to afford results, but the more subtle ones refused to register after two or three repetitions.

He tried two buttons at once to check a theory that breaking the simple rules would count against him. On the contrary, his score mounted. He tried again, with the same result. Thereafter he went back to one button at a time. Obviously on the third or fourth breach of the rule, or possibly just at the end, his score would drop. It was legitimate to test every possibility, but not to follow it out in defiance of the rules. If that were legitimate, the Test itself would be a fraud.

He was wholly concentrated on the struggle with the machine when the buzzer sounded. The score was 3964—his final, irrevocable score, if the Test was to be trusted. Certainly if he took the Test again, at some other center and under a different name, he could operate the buttons more effectively. But then, apparently, the machine would discover by his encephalographic pattern that he had taken the Test before or had been instructed by someone who had. It was an interesting problem.

The girl came in almost immediately and surveyed the score. Raigmore watched her intently. It was perfectly possible that he had achieved a score hitherto regarded as purely theoretical. On the other hand, it was possible that he had done very badly. But if that was the case, he had been set to do an impossible task, lacking the necessary mental equipment.

Sally Morris seemed a little surprised, but by no means startled.

"Well, how did I do?" Raigmore asked, grinning a little anxiously, as he knew people did under these circumstances.

She didn't stall. "Quite well. It will come out in future Tests."

"Have I got this right—I have to take the Tests until you tell me to stop?"

"I or some other operator. Those who drop out at each stage are told the positions open to them, and may take them or not as they wish. But there is nothing open, through the Tests, to anyone whose record is not complete. You may continue any time you wish, here or elsewhere, but to find your position you must continue. In any case, this is a preliminary Test and everyone takes further Tests."

He rose from the chair in the booth. "I may be here tomorrow. Is that all right?"

The girl shrugged. "It's entirely up to you. Today, tomorrow, next year. You obtained your present employment outside the Tests system?"

"I have no present employment."

"Oh, I see. If you have some secret . . ." She paused and fixed him with her eyes, eyes that had a certain power he hadn't noticed before. "It is only fair to warn you that sooner or later the Tests will discover it."

She gave him a green badge. It was an interim badge, to show that he was In Test, no more. Raigmore fixed it in his lapel.

"I wonder," he said.

He had a little of the feeling of curiosity and a tiny flash, a mere impression, of fear. He didn't examine them. He thought that for an instant there had been something wrong with one of the functions of his body. It didn't occur to him then that that had been a moment of supreme significance.

chapter three

CONSIDERING HOW LITTLE RAIGMORE KNEW, IT WAS DANGER-
ous to have anything to do with the Hevers. Raigmore
knew that perfectly well. It was no autocracy, in which a
man like Alexander Hever could be surrounded by men
who could kill and get away with it. No, that wasn't the
danger.

Alexander Hever and his daughter were both White
Stars. It had never happened before like that; Hever's child
was likely to be a White or at least a Yellow, but no family
previously had contained two White Stars in such close
relationship.

To take an important secret into the presence of White
Stars was like carrying petrol through fire. A White Star
had the kind of mind that could work out a whole history
from a single clue. Where a Brown would correlate two
facts and educe a theory, a White Star would link thousands of facts, accept and discard hundreds of theories, go
out for and find precisely the facts he now needed, and
come up with a whole which was stronger than any of its
parts.

Nevertheless, it was essential to Raigmore's plans that he
should bring his existence forcibly to the notice of Alison
Hever and keep it there. She hadn't forgotten him, he could
be sure of that. As far as she was concerned he was, how-

ever, merely a Black with typical Black delusions. It was now necessary to demonstrate to her that he could plan and execute a plan, and to tell her he was In Test. Thereafter she would keep herself informed about him. How he accomplished this was unimportant, so long as it was successful.

He watched the Hever house for the rest of the day. It wasn't ostentatious. Just a house. The guard system, Raigmore noticed again, was only operated to ensure reasonable privacy.

Getting into the house was easy enough for anyone who had the pattern. Anyone, at any rate, with Raigmore's abilities. He had seen three people in the garden. Each of them, during the afternoon, had taken the same route—a curious route which could only mean that there was a selenium-cell network in operation. When it began to get dark Raigmore followed the same route, quickly and confidently, made the same gesture that everyone else had made before the door he had chosen, and went inside. There could have been something he had missed; there wasn't. The essence of really good planning was that the execution was easy and unspectacular to the point of anticlimax.

He spent the evening in Alison's bedroom, waiting patiently. He might have been discovered then—if so, he would merely have identified himself casually as Eldin Raigmore, waiting for Alison, with no explanation as to how he got there, and played the rest as it came.

But no one came near the bedroom. Alison was out at some party—he had seen her go before he walked into the house. She would be late. So much the better.

He read a book until it became too dark. He couldn't put on the light--someone might see it. In the gloom he prowled about, picking up things and peering at them. Anything he could learn about Alison might be useful.

There was very little to learn, however. On one side of the bedroom was a dressing room, on the other a bathroom. Everything was spotless, well designed and comfortable, but there was no evidence of luxury. The homes of Reds, Raigmore knew, were generally full of labor-saving devices. Apparently Whites didn't mind having to rummage in drawers for things instead of having them delivered by chute, or reaching out for light switches instead of controlling them by word commands, or having to soap and dry themselves instead of being washed and dried automatically, without effort, at the touch of a button.

The clothes in the dressing room told him nothing. There were plenty of them, but not enough to indicate vanity or extravagance. No peculiarity of taste emerged. There was a preponderance of informal clothes and sports outfits, but after all Alison was athletic and only twenty-three, so that was to be expected. Even in colors she seemed to have no particular preference. Alison's wardrobe was that of a beautiful girl who was entirely sane about clothes.

Such books as there were about were merely reference books—dictionaries, directories, yearbooks, check lists. There were no odds and ends. The only thing that seemed a little out of place in a bedroom was a coffee percolator. But it was exactly what it seemed to be—Raigmore examined it to make sure.

When at last he heard Alison, Raigmore went into the shower closet off the bathroom and waited there.

After a while she came into the bathroom. He saw her vaguely through the frosted glass and heard her brushing her teeth.

He stepped out silently. "Hello, Alison," he said.

She turned slowly. She was wearing a pale green negligee. Unhurriedly she rinsed her mouth. For all the surprise she showed, she might have known all the time that he was there.

"I've seen you before," she said coolly. "I wonder where?"

But she was merely playing for time. She knew where.

"Ah," she said, admitting it. "The Black—Raigmore. But you're not a Black any more. You're In Test. I suppose you realize that means I can find you afterward?"

He nodded. "Will you want to?"

"Certainly, if only to demonstrate to you that you can't walk into people's houses and hide in their bathrooms like this." She spoke reprovingly, an adult talking to a small, impudent boy. But there was a hint of interest and amusement in her voice. None of fear or anxiety.

"That would need proof," Raigmore observed. "It'll only be your word against mine that I was here. That should count, I know. But in the eyes of the outmoded legal system the word of a White Star is still only the word of an individual."

"You won't even get away."

"I don't agree with you. If I ensure your silence I think I can get away quite easily. But I'd better reassure you. I'm here only to talk. Admittedly, if you screamed I should have to knock you unconscious. But I'm sure you'd scream only as a last resort."

She nodded. "True enough. Screaming ill-treats the vocal cords. Well, while you tell me what you want, let's have some coffee."

"And leave evidence that I was here?"

Alison grinned. "It was worth trying. You don't mind if I have some, do you?"

Raigmore decided she just liked drinking coffee. "Not in the least," he said.

"That's very kind of you. Now what was it you wanted?"

"I want you to take a good look at me. I also want to remind you that one day you'll marry me."

"Oh, Lord," said the girl resignedly.

"You aren't expected to be impressed. You're only supposed to remember."

"You should continue taking the Tests," Alison told him, looking up from the coffee machine. "Then do as the operator recommends."

"That," said Raigmore, "is exactly my intention. Whether psychiatric treatment will be recommended is another matter."

She glanced round at him shrewdly. "You mean there is a purpose behind this apparent insanity?"

"I've given you all the information I intended to give you. Except this. I got in here undetected to speak to you, which is a matter of some difficulty. I am also going to get away without trouble, and you won't be able to prove I was ever here. That's a small demonstration that I'm not just an ordinary Black."

"I had a vague suspicion of that even at the time," she admitted. "You interested me, for some reason. Something different about you. You realize I'll take this as a challenge? If I can find some way of getting you arrested I will."

"Naturally. Don't rely on a lie detector at any trial you can arrange, though. There are ways of getting around a lie detector. You know that."

"Yes, but I find it surprising that you know. Or that you think you can do it."

"It's not the only thing about me that will surprise you. Now I must tie you up and gag you."

Alison laughed aloud. "In such a way that it will look as if I tied myself up?"

"No. With myreline cord, soluble in air."

Myreline was stable for only a short time in air. Oxygen in any mixture, air included, turned it in a short time into a harmless, brittle oxide which fell to dust at a touch. It would leave evidence, but only of myreline—not that Alison had ever been tied by another person.

Raigmore moved swiftly, and Alison opened her mouth to scream. But she was far too late. Raigmore was holding her mouth so that only strangled sounds came out. Most rooms were soundproof anyway.

He had to use all his strength to gag her and bind her without leaving marks which would corroborate her story. He left her on the bed, tied so that she couldn't throw herself to the floor.

"That will hold you just long enough," he said, "for your coffee to get ready."

He was startled when he saw she was trying to laugh. But there was nothing peculiar about the percolator. Apparently he had said something funny by mistake. He would have to study humor more closely.

He got out of the house as easily as he had entered it. It was rather a silly game he had played out. But his whole plan was a game, a game that had to be played under several sets of rules at once, and under certain disadvantages that he had to keep to himself.

chapter four

THE NEXT DAY HE TOOK THE SECOND TEST. IT WAS AGAIN with the buttons; this time it was a memory test. Two hundred and twenty-four of the buttons had to be matched, and the last used to open the door. Sally Morris told him that some people took hours to get out of the booth. If he wished to give up the Test at any time, he was to press a button on the door.

Each button now showed a number on the screen—quite independent of the numbers of the day before. Only one number appeared at a time, and when random or systematic pressing of numbers brought up a number previously noted, both were pressed together and both were eliminated from the test. The object was to eliminate the 112 pairs as quickly as possible, marks coming off when any button was touched more than twice. It was a simple game, but it was designed to reveal a lot.

Raigmore finished it in a little over eleven minutes. He had no marks against him, for he had been patient, taking time to remember and to try to work out a system if it was possible. It wasn't. There was no system, the pairs being arranged in random pattern. Again he could not be sure that he had done particularly well. It seemed on consideration that it could be done in less time. He had taken about 690 seconds, pressing roughly two buttons a second when he hadn't stopped to think. It could be done, theoretically, in five minutes or less. Each button had to be pressed only twice, which meant 450 in all. But on the whole he thought he had done well.

The operator thought so too. She seemed almost excited —as excited as she would ever allow herself to be. After all, she must have a natural desire to see what a superman could do, a wish which inevitably was unlikely to be granted many operators.

Raigmore went straight on to a Test which showed how he handled written instructions, and another which, rather obviously to him, gave him opportunities to cheat which he didn't take.

Then Sally said: "The next item is the physical checkup. After that I can give you an interim rating."

"What does that mean?"

"Nothing much, except that a Purple Star still In Test, say, can't possibly finish below that and probably at least one grade higher. Are you going on now?"

"Yes."

"Shall I call in a male operator?"

Raigmore referred to his mental encyclopedia, which told him that while it was usually left open to people to choose someone of their own sex for medical examinations and things of that sort, only very self-conscious men and women insisted.

"It doesn't matter," he said.

Sally had noticed his hesitation. "I can get one from the central Tests Depot in twenty minutes."

"Never mind."

Test operators were trained to be thoroughly impersonal —so impersonal that it seemed much more natural to call Sally Miss Morris than Sally.

She took him deeper into the Depot and showed him the checkup tank. It was just that, a glass tank two feet deep, seven feet long and four feet broad, filled with a green fluid which was half liquid, half vapor. He knew what to do. He stripped and climbed in, taking the tiny mask that fitted over his nose to enable him to breathe in the tank. Sally warned him not to open his mouth, but he knew that too. There was no secret about this. Knowledge of what was coming didn't make the slightest difference.

The green vapor cut off all sensation. Floating in it, he could feel nothing, not even heat or cold. He sank until he was completely immersed, the liquid supporting him, the vapor covering the rest of him. He didn't have to close his eyes. He could see dimly, as if through thick but flawless green glass.

He knew the process, not in detail, but with general

accuracy. The liquid was a conductor of the P-ray. Where X-rays showed structure, P-rays showed texture as well. This Test would show his health, strength, weaknesses, physical structure, age, blood group, immunities—everything, in fact, that the most rigorous medical examination could discover. If he turned his head, slowly so as not to displace himself, he could see the operator running the various tests and collecting the data from the apparatus.

It didn't take long. The P-ray discovered everything at one operation. Presently Sally tapped the glass to attract his attention, and he climbed from the tank. He wasn't wet. The green fluid was utterly indifferent to the human body.

It was usual for various physical courses to be suggested at this point—suggested only, for the Tests were examinations and entailed no instructions or prohibitions.

But Sally had nothing to say. Raigmore had, as he suspected, that rare thing—the perfect human body. He was a little relieved, all the same. He had thought there was a slight chance that his body, though perfect, might not be perfectly *human*.

All was well, however. The test was exhaustive enough not only to show that he was human but that his children, if he had any, would be just as human as he was. That, he knew dimly, might possibly be important.

Sally left him while he dressed and he found her waiting in a small room off the P-ray Test department.

Silently she handed him a badge.

"You may wear this now if you wish," she told him. It was a purple circle.

Raigmore took it and surveyed it thoughtfully. Millions

of people would give anything short of their lives for the right to wear one of the upper badges—purple, red, orange, yellow, white in ascending order. Anyone who wore any of them was somebody. And he had won it, a stranger, in an hour or so of Tests. Worn with his green badge, it showed he was outstanding and still climbing.

But above the purple circle was the purple cross. And above that the purple star. Then the red circle, cross and star, and so on through thirteen groups to the white star.

The white star that Alison wore.

He had a long way to go yet.

chapter five

THE PROBLEM OF GETTING HIMSELF AN IDENTITY WAS PRESS-ing now. With every Test he took, more about him would be on record. And Sally Morris, to complete that record, would ask questions and expect to get answers.

He had given her the name of his hotel, so it was no surprise when the phone in his room rang and, picking it up, he heard Alison's voice.

"Well, you got away with it, Raigmore, as you said you would," she remarked without preamble.

"I haven't the faintest idea of what you're talking about," said Raigmore.

Every phone conversation was recorded automatically. The police didn't have access to the recording; privacy was highly respected these days. Nevertheless, the recording was made, it must have some purpose, and presumably in some circumstances people listened to it. Very likely the sole reason for Alison's call was to get an admission of some kind by Raigmore on record.

"That was the wrong answer," Alison told him. "You should have pretended you didn't know who I am."

"So I should. Who are you, anyway?"

"Don't let me mislead you," came Alison's voice mockingly. "It can be proved you met me in the elevator the other day."

"Oh, that's who you are. If that's so—hello, Alison."

There was a brief pause. Then a low laugh. "You win, Raigmore," said Alison.

"I hope the coffee didn't boil over?"

She paused again to think that out. "You *are* smart," she admitted. "You know exactly what you can admit and what you can't. In fact, but for one thing I'd even like you."

"What's that—I don't like coffee?" he asked. When Alison laughed again he felt quite pleased. He had thought that might be funny, and so it was, apparently. One form of humor, he knew, was to pick on some phrase or idea or thing and play on it like that. It could be almost anything. Coffee would be a private joke between him and Alison, until it began to wear thin.

"No," she said. "Your stiffness. But perhaps it's wearing off."

She hung up. Stiffness? He thought that out. She couldn't mean physical stiffness. It must be that other stiffness—reserve, lack of ease. If she had noticed that, and didn't like it, it was probably something he should attend to and change if he could. How had he been stiff? It couldn't be just something one felt, like heat or cold—or could it?

Something about the idea seemed to make sense. Sally was impersonal, but she wasn't stiff like . . . like Peach, say— Peach, who was like him. Was that what Alison meant? He thought back and remembered the *stiffness* of Peach. She had behaved like—like a soldier reporting for duty.

Well, wasn't that what she was?

His mind raced on nimbly. This might be very important. It was emotion Alison was talking about, he was almost certain. Emotion was a very puzzling thing. He had plenty of information about it, but none of it made sense, now that he looked at it.

Emotion could be pleasant or unpleasant. There were many kinds of emotion. Fear, anger, enthusiasm, sorrow, all different—and all mere names to Raigmore. He knew what people did when they were afraid, or angry, or enthusiastic, or sorrowful. He could act like that too, if he wished. He could pretend to be afraid, and he knew when to pretend to be afraid.

He could act, in fact, like a highly trained robot.

He got up abruptly. This kind of thinking only gave him the problems without providing any of the answers. What he should do, now that he had time, was look about him, see how people acted and learn some of the things he didn't know. For this *was* important. He could . . . well, feel it. There didn't seem to be a better way to put it.

He didn't know why people did things. What it was like to be angry, afraid or excited. How men and women fell in love. What it was like to be a Brown, for the rest of one's life, with no possibility of ever being anything else. What art was. How life looked to people who had a history, who had been children and who had even, before that, been born. What it was like to remember things, and, remembering them, know they had happened.

The things he didn't know swept over him in a flood, engulfing him. His beautifully orderly brain produced them like a giant machine spitting out cans of food, ten a second, tirelessly.

And though he didn't know it, he was discovering emotion. He was dissatisfied. He was afraid. He was a little resentful. He was puzzled. He felt insecure, anxious, doubtful. He had never felt anything like this before.

He was afraid.

The reaction in him was the same as in any animal. Being afraid, he ran. He slammed the door of his room shut behind him, ran along the corridor, down the stairs and into the street.

Where he would have gone, what he would have done, he had no idea. But outside the hotel someone stopped him and asked for a light. There was something about the way it was done that reminded Raigmore at once of Peach's words: ". . . a woman and a man. But they will introduce themselves to you."

His fear left him and curiosity took its place. Momentarily he was surprised and interested to find how quickly fear could pass. For he knew, now that it was gone, that it had been fear.

The man was speaking. As Raigmore expected, he was

introducing himself much as Peach had done. But this was a Black. Raigmore looked at him closely.

There wasn't much to see. Bill Carter, as he called himself, was just a man, not tall, not short, in no way remarkable to look at. That was a necessary attribute in a spy, of course. The spies of romance with dark glasses and black beards had never existed outside romance. An efficient spy would be one who could hide himself in an instant in a crowd.

The street was busy, and no one was loitering long enough to have much interest in Raigmore and Carter. Nevertheless, Raigmore wanted to get what had to be said over quickly.

"How can I find you if I want you?" he asked.

"I follow you everywhere. Look round for me and you'll find me."

"No," said Raigmore firmly, realizing at once that that was undesirable. "Don't do that. If I need you I'll let you know. Where do you live?"

Carter gave an address. Raigmore didn't write it down. He walked on without another glance at the Black.

The man had shown no resentment, no feeling of any kind, when Raigmore countermanded his orders. Raigmore, Peach, Carter—they were all shadows, Raigmore thought. But he wasn't going to go on being a shadow. He was going to get himself some substance in this world of emotion. He was going to stop being stiff.

He had known all along that he had been human for only a few hours at most before he found himself in the wood four miles from Millo. Memory before that was misty to the point of being incomprehensible. He suspected that the undoubtedly human brain he now possessed was incapable of that kind of comprehension. There had been a world before this one, but it was an unremembered world. Yet it was the unremembered world that mattered. That was axiomatic—there could be no argument about it.

It seemed a little strange that there was no question of divided loyalty. It was supposed to be obvious, apparently, where his duty lay. But he found he wanted to draw his own conclusions. He wanted to see everything, and be able to check it, and know he was right.

He put that thought aside for the moment. His purpose was vague, but nevertheless strong. He was to climb as high as he could in this world . . . and wait. That was all. There were no detailed instructions or even suggestions. He didn't find that part irksome. He would climb as high as he could, doing all that was necessary for him to climb and go on climbing, and he would wait.

Sooner or later the waiting would be over and the whole beautifully ordered picture would be clear.

chapter six

IT WAS LATE AFTERNOON, AND THE STREETS WERE FULL OF people returning from work. Raigmore walked slowly along and really looked at them for the first time. He was one of them. The last Test he had taken said so.

Carefully, like a man who had only just learned about a whole series of mistakes he might have made, he reviewed what he had done, everything he had said. The first step had been to meet Alison—there was nothing wrong with that, but he knew that now he would do it differently. Next, to begin taking the Tests—that was sound enough, for there was urgency about that. Alison again—yes, but already he thought he would do that differently, too, if he could do it again.

It seemed strange that only now was he looking closely at the world he was in.

Everyone wore a Test badge, or practically everyone. Most of the people he saw were Browns. The Browns, after all, were sixty per cent of the population. Perhaps ten per cent were Blacks, who had never taken even the first Test. There was no compulsion. It was certainly expected that everyone at some time or other would take the examination. But people could wait as long as they liked, even till they died. About one in twenty did. The others, including about half of those who wore the black badges now, knew that however well they might get on in the world as Untesteds, they were bound to do better when their capacities were known and trusted.

Curiosity, if nothing else, eventually forced nineteen people out of twenty into taking the Tests. They might be afraid they were Browns. But there was always the possibility that they were Purples, or Reds, or even Whites. As a matter of fact, the people who were afraid of being Browns seldom were.

He saw a few people who, like him, wore the green badge

and another, from the purple circle up. They could wear the double badge proudly. For the Purple wearing the green also might be a future White. Whatever his rank, he was bound to move higher. He might stop at the rank immediately above, or he might go on to the white star.

When the Browns got their badges the Test was complete. So there were no Browns wearing the green In Test badge.

Raigmore found it interesting to watch the reaction of people to the various badges. At other times, his well-stocked mind informed him, special consideration from the people one met had been won by wealth, by aristocracy, by beauty, by strength, by courage. Some of these still ruled. But the principal factor was the badge. A shop assistant wearing the brown would be courteous and helpful to another Brown, but a hint of deference was bound to be added for a Purple or the still higher ranks. Already Raigmore was experiencing some of this deference himself.

A few people wore no badge at all. Most of these would be Whites, Yellows and Oranges. It was not obligatory for the three top groups to wear their marks of rank. It was not that there were special laws for them—it was rather that a White Cross, say, walking in a busy street, would attract more attention than a king wearing his crown a few centuries ago. The fact that the concession covered nine ranks enabled people without badges to pass in a crowd without exciting undue interest. They might be Whites, certainly, but they might also be Yellows or Oranges, or even Browns or Blacks who had lost their badges or forgotten them.

It was illegal for anyone who was not in the three

top groups to appear in public without his badge. Otherwise Browns could masquerade as Whites any time they wished. The police could stop anyone without a badge and arrest him if he couldn't show a white, yellow or orange token.

Raigmore realized, now that he was out of it, that he had been really disturbed for a while. It had been his first encounter with doubt, uncertainty and fear. But now he was beginning to see that the things which had made him uncertain and afraid, though important, were not nearly as big and frightening and serious as he had thought.

Theoretical knowledge could be used as practical knowledge, and when it worked it became practical knowledge. One knew in theory, say, that water frozen became ice, and water heated became steam. One had only to freeze and boil water, and observe exactly what happened, for the dead information to come to life.

No, there was nothing really to worry about in knowing without having experienced.

He built himself up to quite a high level of confidence. He began to experience a new feeling of exhilaration as he looked around him. He was pleased with what he saw; he liked it, it interested him.

So this was emotion. He couldn't remember any emotion before—certainly not before May 23. But then, he could hardly remember anything before May 23.

There was, obviously, good emotion and bad emotion. Content, interest, confidence and satisfaction he liked. They did pleasant things to his body, and his mind basked in them. Fear, doubt, uncertainty and indecision he could just as well do without. But it seemed you couldn't have one lot without the other.

Everyone was healthy, he saw. He knew that hadn't always been the case. People moved briskly, with purpose. They knew where they were going, and what they were going to do when they got there. Everyone seemed to have a goal, and expected to achieve it.

Well, he had a goal too.

The men were conservative in their dress and bearing. They all wore trousers, and some kind of tunic or sweater or jacket or coat. The colors were sober, as a rule—dark blue, dark brown, gray. They walked quickly and cleanly.

The women were more individualistic. The bright colors they wore glinted pleasingly in the late afternoon sun. They wore long skirts, short skirts, slacks, frocks, sweaters, tunics —almost anything, apparently, which took their fancy. At first Raigmore looked at them as he had looked at Alison, admiringly but impersonally, assessing their beauty simply by whether it was pleasant to look at them or not, and quite easily separating the pretty girls from those who were just girls. He noticed that, while there were pretty Browns, the higher-ranking women tended to be more attractive, and decided that was natural, since the girls with more intelligence would make more of any good points they happened to have.

It was only after he had seen many girls join men waiting for them, many couples laughing together, clearly more interested in each other than in anything else in the world, that his mood changed again. It took him longer this time to identify the oppression that came over him, the feeling of desolation that gradually took all the pleasure out of the things he saw.

He got it at last. He was lonely. It wasn't only an emptiness when he realized that all the men his age he saw knew girls they could talk to, girls who might be interested in them. It was a feeling of complete, utter solitude, beyond sex. He couldn't talk to anyone, man or woman. No one would be pleased to see him. He couldn't share his secrets with anyone.

But if the feeling was general, it was keenest when he saw lovers meet. Girls looked at him, seemed to focus their eyes on him for a moment, and then looked past him. One lovely creature in a yellow frock looked straight at him and hurried toward him. He knew her obvious pleasure couldn't be because of him, but his heart raced nevertheless and there was bitter, unreasonable disappointment when she passed within six inches of him as if he weren't there and hugged a small, insignificant youth just behind Raigmore. Raigmore hated the youth. It was no use reminding himself that the girl was only a Brown and that he and she couldn't talk the same language. He wanted to strike down the man she was with and run away with the girl.

It was frightening, when reason returned. He could feel that his body had almost done what he wanted to do. It was tensed, ready for violent action, and he could almost feel his clenched fist striking the youth and the savage satisfaction of it.

In a few hours he had been torn apart, put together and torn apart again by things which his brain told him coldly were of no importance whatever and should not affect him at all. Why hadn't it happened before? If it was because he had had something to do, then the sooner he found something else to do the better. The seesaw of emotion was too much for him.

He started for a drugstore at the thought that he could phone Peach. But before he reached it he knew that wouldn't do any good. Peach was a subordinate. He couldn't confide in her. There was more than that, and he groped for it. She was—like him. Pretending. Not really what she seemed to be at all. She was *cold*.

He wanted the companionship of someone who belonged to *this* world.

chapter seven

THE PLACE WAS CALLED FAIRYLAND, AND IN APPEARANCE AT least it lived up to its name. Though hard drink was served, it was more a meeting place, an open club, than a saloon, and quite a lot of the patrons drank nothing harder than milk shakes. The fairy atmosphere was created more by the lighting than anything else, but the girls who attended the tables helped it. They were dressed as pixies and sprites and flitted lightly and silently about like ballet dancers.

Mirrors softened and broke up the green, blue and red lighting. The hues were never garish or sickly, always subdued, a little unreal, fanciful. The music that seemed to swell out from the walls and rise from the floor was soothing and unobtrusive, but never so swamped by the hum of chatter that it became meaningless. The people in black evening dress and off-the-shoulder gowns looked like guests invited to spend a few hours in a world of fantasy.

Raigmore looked about him like a shy guest forgotten by his hostess. Loneliness had led him here, and it was still with him. He knew he was a stranger; he felt a stranger. He was surrounded by warmth and good humor and laughter and chatter, but he had no part in it.

He took his eyes from the scene as if it hurt them and looked down into his glass. His goal didn't seem to matter much now.

He knew all about alcohol. He knew all the reasons for not drinking it, especially drinking too much of it, but he knew also that people did it. People who had less reason than he had, he told himself moodily.

Obviously he wasn't meant to feel like this. But he did. Whoever put him here had failed. They hadn't taken enough into account. He *must* be meant to know more than he did. Someone, somewhere, had taken too much for granted.

But he couldn't even swear at the someone, blame him for everything, hate him. He knew too little about the someone —it might even be himself.

He tried to picture Alison beside him, laughing, enjoying herself. But the picture wouldn't come.

He looked up again and saw a girl, alone like himself, gliding across the floor. Unlike him, however, she was obviously quite content to be alone—unworried, independent, self-sufficient. She belonged and he didn't. One glance at her was enough to show that she could be alone only by choice.

The unbelievable happened. She slipped onto the seat beside him and smiled at him. "Hello," she said pleasantly.

His spirits soared at once. Even if she left him at once, someone had noticed him, a lovely girl had acknowledged his existence. He saw once more how a tiny thing could alter instantly one's whole attitude to life.

"You look a bit lost, if you don't mind my saying so," she told him, still with that sympathetic smile. She had the gift of being friendly without being brazen. She could afford to make advances without seeming cheap.

"I don't think anyone could ever mind your saying anything," he said, really glad for the first time that he could act his part as if it weren't a part at all. "Say something else. You have a lovely voice."

She raised her eyebrows. "You're not such a wallflower as you look. But don't get the wrong idea. I don't make a practice of picking up people like this."

"I know you don't."

"How do you know?"

He hesitated, afraid of saying something completely above her head, something she would misunderstand. In places like this one missed the badges. People had to wear them in public, and when she went out this girl would have to wear hers, just as she would have to wear something over her shoulders and back. But here hardly a badge was visible. Society, rightly, didn't make informal occasions difficult by insisting that everyone should know at a glance how

44

everyone else rated. Raigmore didn't care whether she was
a Purple or a White—he knew she couldn't be a Brown—but
knowing which would make conversation easier.

"I know," he said rather feebly.

She smiled more broadly. "I know what you're thinking," she said, "but remember, people had to get on somehow for thousands of years without the Tests. Don't let's
become so dependent on them that when someone makes a
witty remark we have to look at his badge before we decide
it's clever."

He laughed. "Well, wasn't that always the case, really?"
he said, trying to talk as he felt. "It's said that people used
to laugh when an acknowledged wit asked them to pass the
salt. I'm sure that before the Tests someone like me talking
to someone like you would be deciding just about now
'The lady has brains, too.' "

"Too?" She smiled. "You mean, as well as you?"

"No. I mean as well as the other things the lady has."

She wasn't a startling beauty, worth a fifth glance, like
Alison. But no one spending an evening with her would
have any complaints. She had creamy arms and shoulders
and had had the unusual sense not to load them with neck-
laces and bracelets and bangles. She didn't even wear a
wrist watch. Her dress was black velvet and could hardly
have been simpler. Her features were delicate and intelligent.

"Let's go over to one of the little tables," she suggested.

They took their drinks and crossed the room, Raigmore
marveling at how easy it was to act and feel like a human
being when he tried. It was almost as if he really was a

human being through and through, despite the fact that his life had only started on May 23. This life, anyway. Perhaps he could forget all about that, for an evening at least. The girl he was with belonged to this world; there was literally a world of difference between her and Peach.

But when they reached the table she had chosen, while Raigmore was thinking this, she said in the same warm, easy manner:

"You should already have met Peach Railton and Bill Carter. I'm Margo Phillips. Still under your orders, like them, but I'm a Red Star. I should be able to help you more than they can."

chapter eight

RAIGMORE STARED AT HER. SHE WASN'T ACTUALLY SMILING, but the smile was there, only a hairsbreadth away. He had to revise a lot of his ideas in a few seconds. "You *can't* be . . ." he murmured.

"What can't I be?" And there it was—the warm, friendly smile that separated her utterly from Peach and Carter. She wasn't playing a part. He could *feel* that she was real in a way Peach wasn't.

But inevitably some of the pleasure of thirty seconds ago was gone. "Oh well, go on," he said. "Say what you have to say."

Now she was looking puzzled. Suddenly terror flashed in

her eyes and she said sharply: "You *are* Eldin Raigmore, aren't you?"

"Oh yes," he said, and the fear died out of her eyes, leaving the puzzlement. "Anyway, so I've been told," he amended. "There have been times in the past few hours when I've wished I were almost anybody else."

"I know the feeling," she said. She let out a long breath, shakily. "I think we feel just about the same, don't we? You didn't expect I'd be like this. And I certainly didn't think Eldin Raigmore would be . . ."

For a moment he wondered if she could be an enemy, a member of some organization fighting him and Peach and Carter. She was human, like Alison, like Sally, like Salter. She couldn't hide that.

But Peach had said "a woman and a man." This must be the woman.

"What did you think I'd be?" he asked.

She didn't answer the question directly. "I've been Margo Phillips for nearly a year. And you've only been Raigmore for a few days. It was months before I began to . . ."

"Why don't you finish your sentences?" Raigmore asked. This was strange and wonderful and was at last beginning to make sense. "You mean for months you were—let's say stiff. Cold. Like a soldier. Like Peach now. You did what you thought you were supposed to do. You planned and waited and took the Tests. Then gradually you began to *feel* things. You didn't like it at first, but after a while you realized you could play your part much better if you really felt what you were pretending to feel."

She was looking at him in wonder. "I knew you were

the leader," she said, "but I was all wrong about what you'd be like. I thought you'd be harder and colder than I ever was. I was afraid . . ."

Raigmore sighed. "I guess it's just one of your habits," he said. "Sometimes I can work out what the end was going to be, but not this time. What were you afraid of?"

She drew a deep breath. "I was afraid that what I said to you could be so wrong that later tonight Peach or Carter would come and see me and . . ."

"And what?" asked Raigmore patiently.

"Kill me," she said simply.

"What for?"

"For feeling. For not being cold and decisive. For being too like the people we're among."

"Meantime," said Raigmore dryly, "you can consider yourself safe. Tomorrow I may change my mind. Things change pretty quickly around here—every five minutes or so."

She laughed. There was relief in the laugh, so much that her laughing got a little out of hand and people turned to stare at her. Raigmore put his hands on her shoulders and pressed until the pain gave her back control of herself.

"Sorry," she said. "I'll go on. There was one job I did have, and it's done, more or less. You need an identity."

"Yes?" He looked at her alertly.

"You also need money, I suppose. I can provide both. Not a lot of money, but you won't need a lot, I suppose— only enough to live on for a while. Is that right?"

He nodded. He had had two hundred dollars on him, no more, when he found himself in the wood. He had been going to ask Peach about funds, when it became necessary.

"I'm a personnel supervisor in a factory," she went on. "It's well paid. The other thing——" She looked a little doubtful, but went on: "I've been working on that for a long time. There's a Black, Joe Banks, who's no good to anyone. He's the same physical age as you and resembles you superficially."

Raigmore interrupted. "You knew what I was going to look like?"

"Yes." She was faintly surprised. Raigmore noted, not for the first time, that all his subordinates seemed to know more than he did. They at least knew about him, and he had known nothing of them.

"Being a Black," she went on, "Banks has no record. No one knows much about him. But I have all the details. Here."

She reached down inside her dress.

Raigmore grinned. "I was wondering why you crackled when you laughed," he said. He took the envelope she handed him.

"You'll destroy that, of course," she said. "But first you'd better learn everything in it. It's your life, remember. You must know all those things."

He put the envelope carefully in his wallet. "And what," he asked, "happens to Joe Banks?"

She looked down at her glass. "You need have no scruple over Banks," she said quietly. "He's not merely worthless, he's dangerous, homicidal. At the moment he's just a petty criminal, but soon he'll murder someone, if he's left alone, and they'll hand him over to the psychologists."

"So I forestall this," said Raigmore bluntly, "and kill him first?"

Still she wouldn't look at him. "It was the only way I could see," she muttered. "I planned this long ago, when I looked on things differently, but I can't see any other way now. If I could . . . But what I said about Banks is true. You'll find it all there. Anyway, I thought . . ."

"You thought murder wouldn't mean anything to me?" She was silent. He frowned. "I have to think about this."

"Ring me tomorrow," she said. "I don't work till the afternoon." She gave him a number and the address of her flat. "Don't say much over the phone."

"I know. I'll take it you can guess most of what I want to say."

He got up. This was business again. It would have to be some other time that he spent the pleasant evening with Margo which he felt could be spent. Some other evening when he was able to forget all about May 23.

He went back to his hotel to think about Joe Banks.

chapter nine

IN THE MIDDLE OF THE NIGHT RAIGMORE WOKE FROM A disturbed sleep and thought: "Of course—I can get Peach Railton or Carter to dispose of Banks." And he went to sleep contentedly.

But in the morning he saw that that was no solution.

There was no essential difference between giving the order and striking the blow that meant the end of another creature's life.

Now that Margo had told him about Banks, the obvious next step was to see the man, at least. He pondered about Margo as he ate breakfast in his room. She was another problem to which at the moment there was no solution. There were too many things to which there was no solution.

Again as he left the hotel someone spoke to him and he found he had another ally. This time it was Jim Fenton, Brown. Apparently neither Peach nor Margo knew about Fenton. Peach had said "a woman and a man"—Margo and Carter. Margo knew about Peach and Carter. Was Fenton some kind of safeguard against Peach and Margo?

Raigmore wondered how many more allies there would be. A Black, a Brown, a Purple and a Red—he had a small but varied army.

Millo was on its way to work. Another branch of the Tests Depot which Raigmore hadn't visited yet was the labor market of this system. People were given jobs which fitted, as near as possible, not only their capacities but their temperaments. They didn't have to take them, but the question hardly ever arose. People knew they would be better off, more suited by jobs found in this way than by any they could find themselves.

For the most part it was possible for everyone to be interested in his job. It wasn't a perfect system yet, but it was well on the way.

Raigmore had scanned rapidly what Margo's notes had to say about Joe Banks. There was a lot there, so much that he didn't want to go to the trouble of memorizing it all until he had seen Banks and decided what to do about him. There was no indication of how she had collected the information. It seemed impossible that she had been able to do it without assistance. A Red Star wasn't in the best position to get information about a Black.

Perhaps she, too, had a subordinate unknown to him. The more he thought about it, the more likely it seemed. He didn't like the idea much; there didn't seem to be much trust and unity in an organization built like that.

He had found the street where Banks lived, however, so he didn't pursue that line of thought.

He had never been in the district before, but he knew about places like this. There would always be an underworld in a culture which allowed a certain freedom of thought. This was it. There would be philosophers and artists here, perhaps a few geniuses; and there would also be criminals, probably known to the police, who would be waiting patiently for an opportunity to order psychological treatment.

It was the sector of the Blacks and the Grays.

The Blacks were Untested, and could be anything. The Grays were the incorrigibles—not the people who could not be adjusted, but the people who refused to be adjusted. People who were sane enough to be allowed to rule their own destiny, but not sane enough to have a demonstrable mental flaw corrected. There were very few of them. It was not uncommon for a man to run up against this block in Tests and refuse to be adjusted immediately. But eventually nearly everyone came round.

It seemed a mean street to Raigmore. But that was comparative. A city of such streets at one time would have been considered a very fine city.

Raigmore, armed with a sketch of Banks's habits, waited for half an hour. People looked at him curiously. He didn't care. If he went through with Margo's plan, he would have to become Banks. It would do no harm if Raigmore had been seen in the vicinity where Banks had lived. In any case, most of the people who passed were Blacks and Grays. The evidence of such people, though not inadmissible, wasn't given a great deal of weight.

Banks duly appeared, and Raigmore followed him cautiously, at a considerable distance. He didn't see the man's face, but from his walk there was nothing to indicate that Raigmore couldn't take over his life. He hadn't expected there would be. Red Stars didn't make mistakes like that.

It was an interesting morning. Banks was on a shoplifting expedition. Raigmore, sometimes quite close to him, occasionally saw the whole operation.

Banks had chosen stores where he was unknown. He would wait outside, learning all he could without going in. And that was a lot, for he chose chiefly glass-fronted stores which afforded a good view of the interior.

When he was ready he would march boldly in, still wearing his badge. Only when he was on the point of stealing the article did he remove the badge, for naturally a Black was a suspicious character, guilty until proven innocent, so to speak. He acted beautifully then, the picture of a White, Yellow or Orange, and made the snatch so deftly that even Raigmore seldom saw it. Then the badge went back on and he was out of the store. On each occasion he bought a heavy, franked envelope, addressed it and mailed it. Raigmore didn't need to see the name and address to know that they were not Banks's own. He would mail the stolen property direct to a fence who could be trusted, at an address which must be constantly changing.

Banks was modest in his thefts. He stole things which were small, things which had considerable value, but nothing in any way spectacular. Several times Raigmore saw him leave something of great value and take instead something which wouldn't be missed for some time, and wouldn't cause a great hue and cry when it was. Most of the things were jewelry of some kind, but he also got away with expensive perfumes, wrist radios, a miniature camera, small ornaments, and valuable electronic components. His job was made easier by the high level of honesty of the population.

Raigmore was wondering how far he could trust Margo's conclusions. She said Banks was vile, worthless, and would be no loss to anyone. Perhaps so—perhaps she, knowing what she had found out for herself, could snuff Banks out without compunction. But Raigmore didn't know these things. To Raigmore, Banks was only a petty thief, no more to be destroyed for that by a conscientious being than the sheep stealers of eighteenth-century England.

Without a clear plan he gradually, subtly allowed Banks to become aware he was being followed. At least it introduced a new factor. Banks would have to do something, and Raigmore wanted to see what it was.

Banks, somewhat incredibly, continued as before after

Raigmore was sure he must know he was watched. But the purpose became clear soon afterward. Following him out of a store, Raigmore found he had lost Banks completely.

The only thing to do, if he wasn't giving up Banks altogether for the time being, was to hurry back to his home by the quickest route and wait for him there.

When, a few minutes later, he heard the step behind him he knew in a fraction of a second that that had been precisely what he was meant to do, and that he had been outguessed by a Black.

Raigmore jerked his head enough to take it out of the path of the blow he knew was coming, but not enough to escape it altogether. A padded blackjack crashed on his shoulder, numbing his left arm.

But as he turned and saw Banks properly for the first time, he was only wary, not afraid. If he was a White or anything like it, and his whole strategy was based on this, he should be a match for any single man, even a man armed with a blackjack.

Then something curious happened. Raigmore tried to read the man's mind. He knew it was impossible, and it *was* impossible—he succeeded no better than if he had tried to fly—but nevertheless he tried it. He did an impossible, stupid, ridiculous thing, and while he was doing it Banks slugged him behind the ear.

Raigmore never completely lost consciousness. He was aware of Banks bending over him, taking his wallet and running. But only then was he capable of movement again, and only because he realized that in the wallet that Banks had were Margo's notes, the notes he should have destroyed.

The Black was welcome to the money, but he mustn't see the notes. They proved nothing, but suggested a lot.

Raigmore should have been dizzy and sick. But the knowledge of what might happen if those notes in Margo's handwriting fell into the wrong hands got him to his feet and running after Banks.

Banks had chosen the place for the attack well. It was a long, curved street that had nothing but blank buildings and walls on either side, with occasional back entrances to warehouses. Running, he must have heard Raigmore's steps behind him, for he turned and waited.

Raigmore never did hear Banks's voice. The Black waited silently, grimly. Raigmore drove in at him and struck at his face. But Banks, though at best he must be badly integrated, was nevertheless a fighter, and an obvious expert. He had the advantage of the blackjack, his criminal experience, and the fact that Raigmore had been slugged twice.

There were no rules. They fought as beasts, with teeth, nails and feet. And Banks had the edge. Raigmore didn't let him land a telling blow, but he couldn't stop him landing a lot of lesser blows that added up gradually but inexorably.

Raigmore started confident, but he became desperate. Perhaps he wasn't a superman after all. Why, anyway, should he be a superman? He had simply assumed it, for no reason whatever. Now it seemed one Black was too much for him. He could hardly feel his left arm at all. Soon Banks would leave him unconscious or dead, and go away with Margo's notes in his pocket.

"Banks!" he shouted suddenly. The Black, startled at hearing his name roared with all the authority Raigmore could muster, tensed automatically and for a fraction of a second was diverted from the job in hand.

Raigmore dived and got his hands on the Black's throat. Though the thief might tear at his back with his nails and claw wildly for his eyes, he couldn't break the grip. It was the first chance Raigmore had had, the only one he needed.

Long after Banks was dead Raigmore kept his grip on his throat.

chapter ten

A CITY LIKE MILLO NOW HAD A MURDER, ONE MURDER, IN ten years or so. A killing like this, discovered, would be the only topic of conversation for days. The police, who could call on all the knowledge and skill of the world for the things that mattered, would seek the killer with a zeal that would separate at once all the people who might have killed Joe Banks from all those who couldn't possibly have killed him. Then it would narrow until . . .

Until Raigmore was caught. It wouldn't mean death for him, but they would restrict him, alter him, and quite incidentally destroy him as what he was.

Raigmore had been lucky in that no one had seen the fight. There would be no advantage in that, however, if anyone came along now.

He carried Banks's body to the nearest recess, a warehouse where the gate was set well back, and left it there while he rushed from entrance to entrance until he found a place where he could leave the body for a little longer. He ran back, lifted it again and bore it to the place he had found. It was an apparently deserted storehouse with a gate low enough for him to get the body over it. He raised it with an effort, let it drop on the other side, and climbed over. A large bin seemed the best place to leave what was left of Banks. He toppled the body in, climbed back over the gate, and carefully traced his way back to where he and Banks had fought.

There was a little blood there, mostly his. Carefully he scraped it away with a handkerchief and a pocketknife.

He was under no delusions about the efficacy of these measures. Should the police suspect there had been a fight in the lane, they could discover almost the whole story in a matter of minutes. But the police weren't to be allowed to suspect anything of the sort.

He had been thinking rapidly. He needed help, and obviously Margo, Peach, Carter or Fenton would have to be called in. He eliminated Carter at once. A Black could be anything. And Fenton, as a Brown, couldn't be entrusted with such knowledge if it could possibly be avoided. He tended toward calling on Peach, since she was less important than Margo and he knew without working it out that she would be less concerned about the fact of murder. But he decided on Margo for two reasons. She knew about Banks already, and could hardly be kept from knowing now that her plan had been carried out. So on the principle of limiting the number of people who knew about the affair, she was the obvious choice. And as a Red Star, she had leisure which Peach didn't have. Peach would come, but others would know; Margo could come without anyone knowing.

He hurried back the way he had come to the first lane and called Margo from the booth at the end of it. If she didn't answer, it would have to be Peach.

She did answer, though.

"Hello, Margo," he said. "Busy?"

He didn't say who he was, and neither did she.

"No," she said.

"Say, have you forgotten you were supposed to pick me up in your car at the corner of Fortieth?"

"No, just coming," she said. Peach might not have had the sense to take what he said for granted.

"I'll be waiting," he said.

He hung up. Yes, he'd been right to call Margo. Peach wouldn't have picked up his meaning like that. If anyone ever listened to that conversation, they were welcome to anything they could glean from it.

She was there in five minutes, a few seconds before Raigmore. He had picked the spot because it was reasonably close to the booth and reasonably far from the place where he had left Banks.

He slid in beside her. "First left, first left again," he said, and the car moved away.

"It's Banks," he went on. "He's dead."

She started, though she tried to conceal it. She also went a little pale.

"I thought so," he said more slowly, relaxing a little for the first time since he had heard Banks's step behind him in the lane. "It was all right in theory, but you don't like it in practice. Frankly, neither do I. But . . ."

He told her briefly how it had hapened. Still she was silent. She wasn't quite as pretty in day dress as she had been the night before, but even more likable, the kind of girl whom almost everyone would like at once, at sight. One felt one wanted to show up well in front of Margo. Raigmore felt that too.

She didn't look in the least like a killer, or a partner in any desperate scheme.

"Well?" he said, an edge in his voice. "Don't you believe me, or something?"

"The way you put it, you had to kill him. Didn't you arrange it so that you had to?"

He opened his mouth to say something angry, accusing, he didn't know what. After all, this was her plan. But instead he had to tell her to stop the car. It had reached the warehouse.

It was dangerous to take a car like Margo's, big and sleek and new, along such a lane, but unavoidable. It was better to take a few big risks quickly than delay and let them multiply. Raigmore preferred one even chance to fifty 100–1 chances.

He jumped from the car, scrambled over the gate, and was back almost at once with Banks's body. Margo didn't look at it. He bundled it into the car and went back to make sure no signs were left.

There was still a plain story in the lane and the bin if anyone really looked for it. He had to trust that they wouldn't, not until it was too late. Next week, say, it would be difficult to reconstruct the story. A month later it would probably be quite impossible.

"Anywhere," he said when he was beside Margo in the car again. "No, go to the wood four miles out on the Lake Oree highway."

The car moved off smoothly. "I'm sorry," she said presently. "I've been very unreasonable. I told you Banks was better dead. It's just——"

"I know," Raigmore said. "I've been wondering if you could be right. Could I have arranged things so that I could delude myself I'd killed him in self-defense?"

He shook his head impatiently. "What's the use? I had to do something like this. We may have to do worse."

"No!" exclaimed Margo.

"Didn't you say you'd do anything I told you?"

She was silent for a full minute. When she spoke it was in a whisper. "I think I'm supposed to."

"But you wouldn't?"

"How can I know? How can you know what you'll do in impossible circumstances? If they happen, you have to do something. But . . ."

"Let's get this over first," he said. "Later we can think about it. But first, let's make sure there's going to be a later. One thing—if my part in this is found out, I'll try to leave you clear. You can carry on."

"Doing what?"

He didn't even try to answer that.

Before they left the city Raigmore bought a small excavator. There was no further trouble. At the spot he pointed out, a place he remembered, Margo turned the car off the road. The ground was rough, so broken up that the car would leave no trace. Nevertheless he carried the body a hundred yards farther into the wood to bury it. First he cut the turf carefully and piled it on one side; then he set the little machine to work and it threw the gravel to one side in a fine spray. When Banks's body was ten feet underground, the turf carefully replaced and the mold and bracken and twigs kicked back over it, even Raigmore, looking back, could hardly pick out the exact spot.

Disposing of a body was never too difficult if one was careful to avoid overelaboration.

chapter eleven

MARGO TOOK OVER WHEN THEY GOT BACK TO MILLO. SHE HAD worked out what had to be done if Raigmore was to replace Banks. Raigmore knew she would have done it efficiently, and meant to do as she said without question.

He was now almost certain she couldn't have found out all she knew about Banks unaided. She knew about Peach and Carter, but didn't seem to know about Fenton. Presumably she also had a private ally, a Brown or Black or Purple, who served her alone. He didn't ask. This wasn't the time for such questions.

"We'll need Peach," Margo told him.

"Must she come into it?" he asked, violating his own rule.

"If she doesn't, I'll have to take risks myself. I don't mind that particularly, but I think they're risks that Peach is meant to take. She's expendable."

Raigmore didn't answer. She turned to him sharply. "What's the matter?"

"You're two people," said Raigmore. "One of them planned the murder of Banks. The other was horrified that I'd done it. The first one talks about Peach being expendable. The other may call me a callous, unfeeling monster if anything happens to Peach."

Margo began desperately "But we've got to——"

"So that's it. The first one comes out for emergency. She'd have killed Banks herself. And you're Margo I again—is that it?"

She looked hounded. "No. I hate this. It's got to be done. Leave me alone to do it, will you?"

"I'm sorry," he said, and meant it. He phoned Peach. It was her lunch hour by this time. In these days of short hours her lunch hour extended to two and a bit. He merely allowed her to recognize his voice and told her where he was. There was no need for more.

She was there in ten minutes. Raigmore said nothing, but nodded to Margo.

Margo had herself strictly under control again as she gave Peach her instructions. If Banks didn't claim what the fence owed him, that man, criminal though he might be, would know Banks was dead. Peach had to go and collect it, representing herself as from Banks, proving she knew him well, hinting though not stating that Millo had become too hot for him after that morning's work and he was leaving it or had already left it.

When she had done that she was to visit various addresses which Margo gave her and pay what Banks owed the people who lived there.

"Be as hard as you can," Margo told her. "We don't know what Banks owes. You have to pretend you do, but let them see you don't—he's left in too much of a hurry to tell you. Whatever they say, try to beat them down, but pay the lowest figure you can agree on."

Peach nodded. She accepted the instructions as indifferently as if Margo were sending her across the street for cigarettes. "Banks is dead, of course," she observed.

"The less you know the better."

"Naturally. But why pay at all? Is this Banks the kind who would?"

She was merely asking for information which would enable her to play her part better. Margo acknowledged the point. "Not if he could help it," she said. "It's a question of what his associates will believe and what they'll do. If they're not paid what Banks owes them, they might, in revenge, drop clues about Banks to the police. Banks would know that. Banks would pay. So you pay with bad grace, but so that they'll forget Banks. Is that clear?"

"Women?" asked Peach.

"He just broke with one girl. She doesn't matter. You're supposed to be his new girl."

"Name?"

"Peach Railton," said Margo. "You're the connecting link between Banks and Raigmore. Banks is Raigmore now."

That was all Peach wanted to know. "Ring me at my flat

at half past two exactly if everything goes as arranged," Margo said in conclusion. "I won't answer, but I'll hear it. If you don't ring, Raigmore or I will get in touch with you."

They both looked at Raigmore for his assent to all this. Even though Margo was trying hard to be cool and businesslike, there was still a world of difference between them. Peach was a hard, trained soldier waiting for confirmation of orders, and though she wore her plastic dress, which should have made her look at least interesting, Raigmore found it quite impossible to think of her as a woman at all. Margo, in a gray, beautifully cut frock, couldn't help being warm and attractive as ever, and, womanlike, was looking at him anxiously, hoping on the one hand that he didn't think she was really like this, and on the other that he thought she had done well. *Mary, Mary, quite contrary,* he thought, and almost laughed.

"Carry on," he said.

When Peach had gone he told Margo: "I wish she hadn't had to be brought into it."

They were on their way to Margo's flat to wait. "Why not?" she asked.

"Now Peach knows one of us killed Banks. And that I'm supposed to have been Banks before I was Raigmore."

"It doesn't matter. The rest of what she knows about us anyway is far more important."

"It *does* matter," Raigmore insisted. "The other thing is vague, hazy and incredible. This is a civil offense."

"Are you dissatisfied with how I've handled this?" she asked raggedly.

Raigmore shut himself up abruptly. He realized the strain on Margo, the responsibility she felt for the success of her plans. It wasn't fair to worry her further.

Margo's flat was as luxurious as might be expected of a Red Star. That is, at about the top level of luxury. Alison's rooms hadn't been pretentious—Whites hadn't much time for pretentiousness. The Reds were the richest of all the groups. For they were the last group, in ascending order, who cared about wealth as wealth.

Raigmore knew that Margo's job as a personnel supervisor would be very highly paid, would take up very little time, and would demand the full capacities of a Red Star.

They didn't speak as they waited. Raigmore, who was rapidly learning about people and particularly Margo, knew she wanted him to speak but would snap at him, whatever he said. She kept looking at the clock.

The Reds were the only group that had pronounced common characteristics. They loved luxury, they were impatient, and yet they were good at handling people. Placed midway, they could get on with and understand Browns and Purples, yet they had the intelligence, sensitivity and self-confidence to understand and work well with Oranges, Yellows and even Whites. From some points of view they were the most useful and likable group.

Margo had most of the characteristics. Whatever she had been before becoming Margo Phillips, or even in her first few months in Millo, she was a Red Star now, with all that that implied. And Raigmore liked her.

Things might have been different, he reflected, if he had met Margo before he decided coldly that he must marry

Alison if he could. But perhaps not. He found himself unwilling, for some unknown reason, to pursue that line of thought.

Margo moved restlessly. Raigmore looked at his watch. The minute hand was a fraction from the half hour.

The phone bell rang.

Margo sighed and relaxed visibly. "Now," she said briskly, "I have to go and work."

Raigmore laughed. A moment ago she had been jumpy, ready to snap at anything. Now she was herself again. It was typical Red Star volatility.

chapter twelve

SALLY MORRIS LOOKED UP FROM THE PAPERS IN FRONT OF her. "This was a word test, of course," she said. By this time she was talking quite freely about most of the Tests and their purpose. It was only to be assumed, from the way he performed them, that Raigmore could guess pretty accurately the principles behind most of them—at any rate, after he had done them. "It's meant to test the clarity of your concepts, the suitability of the symbols you use for them, and the emotional content of these labels for you."

Raigmore nodded. But he was wary suddenly. He had known all about the first two things, but had been only dimly aware of the third.

"In the first two," Sally went on, "you're optimum—that is, as good as the Test itself. In the third . . ."

"Something unusual?" said Raigmore lightly.

"Very. In some cases you've used the symbols purely logically, mathematically. That's not strange. Some of the members of the higher groups train themselves to be able to do that with all symbols when they like, consciously, deliberately—it helps them to be completely rational. But to others you react highly emotionally. That's not strange either. What is strange is the imbalance."

She was inviting an explanation. Raigmore knew by this time that she was intelligent and highly trained. He guessed, too, that he was In Test all the time he was with her, not merely when he was performing the individual items.

"And I suppose," he observed, "that the symbols with strong emotional content are those concerned with the basic instincts?"

"Right. You know why?"

"No. Except that my life has been rather strange, as you must know by this time."

"In what way?"

He was silent. She shrugged her shoulders. "It's your right not to tell me, of course. The Tests are enough."

"Exactly," said Raigmore. "I stand by the Tests."

"To put it generally—the Tests will prove you right or wrong, and you want to wait and see?"

"Yes, that's it."

"That's reasonable. But I must ask you some questions now. And if you continue, you have to answer them."

She fired scores of questions at him, and let him see that

those which were not answered at once were marked blank. Age? Sex? Race? Religion? What were women? How long did he mean to live? Where was Egypt? What was pi? Had he ever been in love? Were Swedes better than Italians? Did he think she, Sally Morris, was pretty? How far was it from New York to San Francisco? What was the first thing one noticed about Mars when one landed there? Did he believe in God?

He had to decide in the middle either to put up new, comprehensive blocks or to tear them all down. He tore them all down and answered the big questions with whatever came. Only on points of personal history, and there weren't really many of them, did he take in facts that applied to Joe Banks, or could apply to Banks, and not to him.

The questions went on and on. Who was nice? What was truth? How many people were there in Millo? What color did he like best? Who was Alexander Hever? When did one know someone was lying? Did he like children?

Sally didn't have a list of questions. The things she asked were affected by his answers, but not obviously, not directly. She handled the interrogation superbly, keeping him intent on the question of the moment. She seemed to know exactly when he realized that what she was writing down was of no importance whatever, and stopped doing it. The session, of course, would be recorded in sound and examined later.

Was it better to jump right or left? Did he like spaghetti? Who was the greatest criminal of history? What was it like to be beaten at something? When did Mark Twain live? What did he think of this Test?

It was only after he had said briefly: "I'm not thinking about it," after the fashion of his other answers, that he understood he was supposed to elaborate on this one.

"I've just been trying to give the first thing that comes," he said. "Sometimes that isn't easy, though the concept is clear enough. How long do I mean to live? I said as long as I can, but that was just what I thought was a reasonable answer. I don't mean to live any set time."

"Does that answer the question?"

"No, the first thing I said was the answer. I'm not thinking about it because . . ."

"Are your reasons part of the answer?"

"No, but they explain it."

"Why do you want to explain it?"

"I like to explain most things, I suppose."

"Why?"

"To invite agreement?"

"Why do you want agreement?"

"To justify myself, I suppose."

"Why do you say 'I suppose'?"

It went on until Raigmore felt limp, squeezed dry. It seemed that he had tried to answer every question that could possibly be asked.

Sally smiled at him suddenly. He smiled back, a little uncertainly.

"Where do I see this psychologist?" he asked.

"You don't. Not yet, anyway. Remember the Tests and the psychological treatment that may go with them are not meant to iron out the differences in people. You're unusual in a lot of ways, certainly. But there has been nothing to suggest that you're not sane."

Raigmore pondered over this. "Could a White Star be eccentric?" he asked.

"Every White Star is eccentric. Eccentric means not placed centrally."

"But I mean—could a White Star be fanatic about, say, the proper diet for babies of three months?"

"Certainly. White Stars, like the rest of us, set up goals for themselves out of their experience. We may not see why they pick them, why they should be so concerned about things like that, and we may call them fanatics. But since they're White Stars, they'll be effective. They'll be effective even though the means they choose may not seem to lead even in the direction of their end."

Raigmore nodded.

"Your own major problem," said Sally casually, "may resolve itself without any trouble. You don't know what you are. You're still a little afraid to feel, not knowing what you ought to feel. You're cautious with people, not knowing how much of yourself to give. You have big plans, and don't know if you're big enough to carry them out."

Raigmore tensed, feeling he had suddenly been stripped of all pretense and was trapped, naked, before her.

She smiled slightly. "It shouldn't really surprise you, if you think about it," she said, "that in this you're exactly the same as nearly everyone else at this stage."

Before he left the Depot she asked him the name of a girl he knew.

"What for?" asked Raigmore cautiously.

"I'm not going to tell you exactly, of course. Generally—if we kept testing people only individually we might miss things which would be obvious if we saw how they behaved in society. Later we'll see you with groups."

Raigmore nodded. "This girl—what should she be like? Am I supposed to know her well, or hardly at all, or what?"

Sally shrugged her shoulders. "As you like. She should be an attractive girl, someone you like, a girl whose Test record is complete, and preferably not a Brown. That's all. We'll get in touch with her and ask her to co-operate. She doesn't have to, but probably she will. You're not supposed to communicate with her before you meet her here."

She smiled. "You're not committed to marrying her or anything like that. Does that cover it?"

"I suppose I can't pick you?"

"No, I'm afraid not. Try again."

He would have given Margo's name at once, but some little thing might come out that shouldn't.

"Alison Hever," he said boldly.

Sally started to shake her head again, then looked at him sharply. "She asked once about you. You know her, then?"

"I've met her."

"All right, I'll ask her. But White Stars usually don't . . . can you give me someone else, in case Miss Hever refuses?"

He didn't even consider Peach. "Margo Phillips," he said.

chapter thirteen

HE DIDN'T TRY RINGING MARGO, THOUGH HE WOULD HAVE liked to warn her. Any attractive girl, Sally had said. It wouldn't be merely a straight sex-reaction experiment. There was nothing so elementary at this stage of the Tests; besides, for anything like that they would have girls at the Depot, actresses, doing a job.

He wouldn't have thought about it any more than any of the other Tests but for two things. He knew he might be startlingly abnormal on sex, never having had time for it in his brief life as a human; yet such thoughts as he'd had, such attitudes as he could discover in himself, seemed normal enough when he compared them with his encyclopedic knowledge. The second thing was that the girl concerned would be either Alison, White Star, or Margo, half human. He wished he had known some ordinary girl, any girl but the only three he knew.

However, since there was nothing he could do about it, he arrived unconcernedly enough for the Test. "Just go in there," said Sally, "and talk."

"Who is it?"

She merely gave him the grin that meant Nothing doing.

The room she had indicated, he saw at a glance, was bare but for two chairs. And the girl, he saw in the same glance, was Alison.

"Hello," she said. "Red Cross now, and still climbing? Perhaps I'll have to marry you yet." The same irony was there, but it was tinged with interest and curiosity.

"I haven't told them about that here," he said. "What are we supposed to do? Just talk, for the recorder?"

She wore a black skirt and white blouse and was magnificent. She also wore her white star, perhaps to put him in his place.

She sat on one of the chairs and crossed her legs. "By a curious coincidence," she remarked, "this part of the Tests was started as a result of a suggestion I made in my Test thesis. So I know its purpose pretty well. The question is, can you tell me what it is?"

"Don't I get any further information?"

"You shouldn't need it."

"Then this is an opportunity for me to put on a show. To show off, in fact. It can't be anything else."

"That's good," said Alison, not hiding her pleasure that he had got it right. "That's really good. Explain it."

"If you could be any attractive girl, and this is a Test, all that's possible for me is to show off in front of you. To exhibit my male superiority, if I can."

"Very well," said Alison with her ironic grin. "What kind of show are you going to put on?"

"I'm going to assume this is a fair test, that you're presenting me with material that you're supposed to present, that it differs depending on the people involved, and say you lied when you said you introduced this Test."

"You are?" inquired Alison with raised eyebrows. "Why?"

"Because White Star theses are entirely concerned with the top range and this is obviously no higher than Red level. If you want me to explain 'obviously,' I——"

"No. Tell me what you're going to do next."

"I'm going to wait until you present me with something else. You haven't given me it yet."

They went on talking for twenty minutes. Alison played her part well enough, but never pretended she was doing anything other than playing a part. She gave him his cues and he missed only one of them. He was a little preoccupied after that, wondering how serious it was.

But at the end, which Alison indicated plainly and quite honestly, she said: "I'm glad I came, Raigmore. You were almost too good."

"Is that possible?" he asked.

"Oh yes. There are supposed to be failures, so that you can think about them and be bothered by them. You were supposed to miss three things. But don't let's talk here. Come out for a few minutes and have some coffee."

They didn't see Sally as they went through the Depot. "Do you own a coffee factory or something?" Raigmore asked.

She smiled. "Some people doodle. Some whistle between their teeth. I just drink coffee."

They went into a cafeteria opposite the Depot. "The Test isn't over," Alison said. "We'll go back in a few minutes."

"Alison," said Raigmore earnestly, "I'm sorry about what I said and did earlier. I——"

"Oh," said Alison lightly, "this Margo Phillips is a rival, is she?"

"I didn't mean that. Anyway, what do you know about Margo?"

"When Sally Morris asked me to come along today I asked if you'd named anyone else, if I didn't come," Alison told him candidly. "I'd probably have said no, but when she mentioned Margo I said I'd come. You can say 'Just like a woman' if you like."

Raigmore raised his eyebrows. "Am I allowed to draw any conclusions from that?" he asked.

"I can't stop you. What's Margo Phillips like?"

"Very nice. But what's the use of telling one woman about another woman?"

Alison smiled. "Come on, Solomon," she said, getting up, "there are more Tests. But don't ask me about them."

"I wasn't going to. I don't think I have to be scared of the Tests."

"No," said Alison. "I don't think you do."

The other Tests with Alison were mere relaxation. That was quite frankly what they were. The Tests took in a lot of territory, and that included how people played as well as how they worked, thought and talked.

Sally took them to a room that had a dance floor and a phonograph and told them to dance and make conversation. She left them to it. Raigmore had learned in the first few days, as a matter of course, to swim, dance, jump, skate and a dozen other things which he had known how to do but had never, to his knowledge, actually done. In every case it took only a few minutes, since he knew exactly what to do and had excellent control over his body.

He enjoyed dancing with Alison. Presently he began to realize that he wanted to come out high in the Tests, other things apart, simply because then he might win her. He liked Margo, but Alison . . .

"When I said you were stiff," she murmured, "I must have been thinking of two other fellows."

Then they were given copies of a play and asked to learn and act a scene. By this time they were treating the whole thing as a game. Alison acted very well; Raigmore's performance suffered because he was more interested in her than in what he was doing.

In another episode, unscripted this time, Raigmore had to scrape acquaintance with Alison on a beach. Raigmore had changed into trunks and was pleasantly surprised to find Alison in neat white shorts and a green halter, to add verisimilitude to the scene. There was no acting in his ardor—she was exquisite. Sally had some difficulty in breaking up that incident.

Through half a dozen other episodes Raigmore moved easily and contentedly. The only time he remembered that there was anything peculiar about him he pushed the thought well out of sight. The Tests said there was nothing peculiar about him.

At the end Sally took back Raigmore's red cross and handed him an orange circle. He had jumped Red Star rank completely.

"That was the pleasantest double-jump I ever made," he said. "Let's do it again and I'll be an Orange Star."

Alison was looking at him thoughtfully. The lightheartedness of the Tests was gone; there was a new seriousness in her manner.

Perhaps she was realizing for the first time it was quite likely that the next time Raigmore told her she was going to marry him it wouldn't be a joke any more. Or perhaps—after all, she was a White Star—she had realized that a long time ago.

chapter fourteen

THE NEXT DAY SALLY INTRODUCED RAIGMORE TO FRED SALTER.

"You're the crazy man who wants to marry Alison," Salter said.

Raigmore looked at him sharply, but no offense seemed to be intended. Fred was a lazy, good-humored fellow—too lazy and good-humored, Raigmore soon decided. He was into the Orange, but Raigmore guessed he wouldn't go much further. The top groups had to have drive, which Salter lacked. At least, which Salter often lacked. He would work hard enough at a thing, but would relax into inactivity at the earliest opportunity.

Raigmore and Salter often had to compete from then on, and they had plenty of opportunity for getting to know each other. The purpose of the competition wasn't entirely clear, for the result was almost always stalemate.

The atmosphere of the Tests, curiously, was easier toward the top. Salter and Raigmore and Sally talked quite openly and cheerfully about each Test and its purpose. Raigmore discovered that it had been only by chance that he happened to have Sally as his operator from the start. She was a Red Circle, quite capable of running the Tests to the top. Salter had started with a more ordinary operator and had only recently been passed on to Sally.

Salter and Raigmore were again asked to name two girls, and as Alison was out of town Raigmore named Margo. Salter had named Gloria Clarke. The four of them were at the Tests Depot all day, doing all kinds of things, things difficult and easy, things in which they all took part, things in which three watched the other, contests in pairs, individual contests. The girls, being already rated, formed a sort of anchor.

During a break when the girls were changing their clothes, Salter remarked: "I like Margo. Why don't you marry her?"

"Because I can't see any reason to marry a girl you like."

Salter laughed. "Fair enough. But do you really mean it? Suppose I took her out, say. Would it be pistols at dawn?"

"You take Margo out?" Raigmore asked. "What about Gloria?"

"Gloria's practically a cousin," Salter protested.

Raigmore understood. Once people started regarding each other as relatives, marriage was definitely out. It didn't matter how near or how distant the relationship was. If a man said a cousin wasn't really a very close relative, he might be thinking of marrying her. But if he said his aunt's husband's second cousin's daughter was a relative, he certainly wasn't.

When the girls joined them, the four of them argued about the Tests system, with particular reference to the one which was going on at the moment.

"This society-test business," Salter observed, "is probably just a check on social aberrations. To see if we stand on our hands and clap our feet whenever we meet a red-headed man, for example. If we do, then possibly there's something wrong with us, you never know."

"It all seems very empirical," said Gloria.

"Must be empirical," Salter asserted lazily. "On the basis 'This is what Reds ought to be able to do.' And gradually it gets absolutely perfect lower down, and nearer perfect at the top."

"I don't see that it *need* be so empirical," Raigmore argued. "You can test deduction, induction, imagery and so on in such a way that you could be working far ahead of anything that has ever been achieved. 'If there were a group beyond White Star, they should be able to . . .'"

"It's far too unemotional," Margo declared. "Emotion is the basis of art. Art demands talent. Talent isn't the same as intelligence. So the Tests discover all the abilities on the thinking side, and only some on the feeling side."

"We don't know what they discover," Salter declared. "We're prodded from behind and made to shuffle sidewise, never knowing what's coming and never quite sure where we've been. But don't think I object. I love it. Put down a good mark for that, Sally."

Sally wasn't there. But what they were saying was presumably being recorded.

"The Tests must be an education as well as just an examination," said Raigmore. "Look at that last one. It hasn't any purpose except showing you and me, Salter, that there's some things at which the girls can beat us hollow."

"And testing how you took it," Margo added.

"And seeing how long it took you to reach that conclusion," Gloria observed.

"And perhaps even," contributed Salter, "showing us a weakness with the idea of finding out later whether we've done anything about it. So you see, Raigmore, you're all wet, as usual."

Salter and Raigmore were rather shocked, too, to find in how many of the physical tests Margo and Gloria were their equals or even superiors.

"That's another old axiom that we're finding out isn't an axiom," said Gloria. "For so many thousands of years women knew they weren't as good as men at these things, and men knew it, that it was only gradually the idea could be broken down. The record for the women's hundred yards used to be over eleven seconds. Why, at school they expected us to do better than that."

They were very pleased with each other, and admitted it. At the higher levels there was so much understanding, such diversity that a Red Star like Margo wasn't out of her depth with even a White—not nearly as much as, say, a Brown would be with a high Purple. The Reds were integrated, knew what they didn't know, and weren't bothered by it.

But later, when Raigmore saw Margo home, she was troubled.

"I like these people," she said. "But we're working against them, aren't we?"

"Are we?" Raigmore asked. "Do you know anything that shows we are?"

She waited, hoping he could reassure her.

"We can't belong to a ruthless race," Raigmore went on. "I didn't want to mention Banks again. But I haven't been able to forget him. He's dead, and I'm not crying every night about it. But I don't think I could ever kill anyone again, anywhere, in any circumstances, for any reason. The Tests say I can't, did you know that? Same for you. No Red or higher could kill except in self-defense, Sally tells me. Let's trust the Tests."

She smiled. "I don't know whether I'm believing that because I want to believe it," she said. "But I think you must be right. We *couldn't* belong to a ruthless race."

chapter fifteen

FOR LONG PERIODS NOW RAIGMORE WAS FORGETTING THAT there was anything strange in his life. He spent most of his time with Salter, either in the Tests or after them, until Salter stuck. He was a Yellow Circle. Nothing he could ever do would raise him among the top five classes. But he was content. He hadn't dared to hope until recently that he would achieve the Yellow. Roughly, in the Purple you were one in twenty, in the Red one in two thousand, in the

Orange one in a hundred thousand, and in the Yellow one in a million. Numbers ceased to have meaning when you came to the Whites. One generation would have twenty White Stars. The next would have only twenty Whites altogether. You couldn't calculate geniuses by numbers. And the White Stars were versatile geniuses.

But when Salter stopped, Raigmore was working through the Yellow. Sally Morris was becoming alternately wildly excited and awed, and showing it. With the population at its present level, it fell to very few Test operators to find a White. For they could be found only once. She would have something to talk about for the rest of her life, and people would always listen. Perhaps, after years of repetition, she would prevaricate a little and say she had known it from the moment Eldin Raigmore walked into the Depot. But probably, as befitted a Red, she would admit to the end that it was only in the last week that it even occurred to her that he was in the top four groups.

Raigmore had admitted to being Banks. That is, he had grafted most of the history of Banks onto his and it was accepted as fact. It was enough. He didn't need a detailed record, but there had to be something more than a vacuum behind him.

He still spent a lot of time with Salter. Usually Gloria would be with them, sometimes Margo. Occasionally, not often, Alison would join them. She never referred to the first two occasions on which she had seen Raigmore. While Raigmore was still In Test, the affair was *sub judice*, so to speak. When all five of them were together she behaved, unself-consciously, as if she were odd girl out, Gloria with

Salter, Margo with Raigmore. Salter complicated this by behaving as if he were with Margo and Raigmore with Alison. And Gloria looked on with the cool amusement of a Yellow Star.

Margo spoke about it once when she and Raigmore were waiting in a box at the theater for the other three.

"Do you think she will marry you?" she asked. She couldn't keep it from sounding a little wistful; Raigmore had known for some time that she was in love with him, or thought she was. She hadn't really noticed Salter's attentions yet.

"I don't know," said Raigmore. "Margo, I'm sorry."

"What about?"

"Don't let's start pretending at this stage," he said quietly. "Even if I loved you, I wouldn't marry you. Perhaps we'll never be called on to do anything, you and I, but wait. I hope so. In any case, I'm certain we were never meant to marry each other. Others, yes. If we are spies of some kind that's a good way to hide."

"I wish I knew!" she said passionately.

"Knew what?"

"I don't even know that. But . . ."

The other three came in together. Salter sat behind Margo and began to talk to her animatedly, over her shoulder.

The play was *As You Like It*. Alison, who sat on the other side of Raigmore, was surprised that he had never seen it acted. He might have added that he had never, to his knowledge, read it; nevertheless, he knew what it was about and some of the purple passages from it.

The house lights went down. "I acted Rosalind at school," Alison whispered. Raigmore wondered what kind of school a White Star could go to. But then, of course, she couldn't be known to be a White Star until she'd left school, though quite a few people must have had a good idea by that time.

Raigmore couldn't get his mind on the play at first, for some reason. He didn't know why he should be uneasy, but he certainly was. He couldn't work up any interest in Orlando. Even when Rosalind and Touchstone appeared he could only follow what was going on without enthusiasm. Alison, on his left, seemed to sense his mood. He was aware of her looking at him several times. On his right, Margo was aware of nothing but the play. She was living it—once or twice he looked at her and saw her face, expressive as a child's, in the reflected light.

"You don't like poetry?" suggested Alison as the lights went up at the end of the act.

"Yes, but . . ." He shook his head.

"Something wrong?"

"I don't know."

In the second act, however, when Rosalind appeared in boy's clothes, the play began to grip him. He wondered how Alison had played Rosalind. The boy's clothes would have suited her. She had the essential femininity that made all kinds of masculinity possible without detracting from her appeal. Without ever seeing it exhibited, he had realized that courage was the key point of her character. Once that was understood, everything else about her fell into place. Her coolness when he might have been an assassin or a madman—it wasn't indifference, emotionlessness, failure to appreciate the circumstances. It was the whipcord resilience of a girl who could not possibly be broken. She could be destroyed but never bowed.

And she would take a long time to get to know. She wouldn't give herself all at once, as Margo did. The warmth was there, but deeper. It would be a slow, wonderful business getting to know Alison.

He lost himself more and more in the play, like Margo, until suddenly Jacques spoke the oftenest-quoted lines from it, lines familiar to Raigmore, though he never seemed to have heard them, but with more significance than he had ever thought they could have:

> *"All the world's a stage,*
> *And all the men and women merely players:*
> *They have their exits and their entrances;*
> *And one man in his time plays many parts . . ."*

He had a wild thought that he and Margo and the others had wandered into the wrong play by accident, onto the wrong stage, to the wrong world. That their entrances and exits were being acknowledged by the other players, but only so that some vast, unseen audience should not suspect that there was anything wrong. And some mightier Shakespeare, some celestial stage manager, was watching them closely, prompting his players so that . . .

Someone had come in and was bending over Alison. Amiens was singing:

> *"Heigh-ho! sing, heigh-ho! unto the green holly:*
> *Most friendship is feigning, most loving mere folly."*

Alison was getting up quietly. Behind her Salter and Gloria rose, questions in their faces. Raigmore had to take Margo's arm before she noticed anything. Together they left the box and went out into the foyer. The man who had spoken to Alison had disappeared.

"My father's dead," said Alison. "Murdered."

"Oh no!" exclaimed Margo.

"I want someone to help me," Alison said. No one thought it strange that she looked at Raigmore. "I'm not sure I'll be able to think quite straight. I'm going to see the man who did it."

"Would you rather we didn't come too?" asked Salter.

"Take Gloria home, Fred. I'll ring her later, or perhaps Raigmore will come over afterward."

Gloria and Salter took Margo with them. Raigmore drove Alison's car. He left it to Alison whether she talked or sat in silence. He wasn't thinking anyway. He couldn't think. He knew dimly that Margo would be even more dazed, but it didn't seem to matter whether Salter and Gloria noticed it or not.

They didn't see Hever's body. The killer was an insignificant Brown named Edward Brolley. He didn't seem to know what was going on or where he was.

"See if you can get anything out of him," said Alison. The police were there, but the police didn't have Whites they could call on at a moment's notice. The Hever house was a buzz of people who felt they had to rush about and do something, but didn't know what to do.

Raigmore spoke to the man quietly, soothingly. Alison disappeared for a moment. There had been a tiny spark of recognition for an instant, as if Brolley had at least seen Raigmore before, but no one except Raigmore noticed it. Perhaps it had been part of Brolley's job to pick a time when Raigmore couldn't be suspected of implication in the crime.

When Alison came back he told her: "It's not an act. He's absolutely mindless. The only thing to do is hand him over to the psychiatric division at the Tests Depot."

"Will they get anything?"

"I don't think so. It's not any kind of compulsion imposed on a weak but sane mind. Do you know of any possible prior connection between him and your father?"

"None. Then it's meaningless?" Some of the feeling she was strangling showed in the way she spoke the last word.

Raigmore hesitated. "Meantime, yes."

"What do you mean, meantime?"

"If anything else happens, it won't be."

Her off-the-shoulder evening dress was incongruous among so many uniforms. "There must be something the psychiatric division can get from him, if there's any purpose behind it," she said with a vehemence that seemed impossible for her.

Raigmore hesitated again.

"Say it," she said. "That's why I brought you along."

"If there is a purpose, the fact that Brolley's alive and in police hands shows he knows nothing. No party who have any reason to wish your father dead would permit their agent to be captured and have his brains picked."

There was nothing more he could do. He wasn't unduly concerned about Alison. If a White Star couldn't handle the tragedies of life, who could? He was much more concerned about Hever, whom he had never met.

He told Salter and Gloria all there was to tell, and then took Margo home.

"I suppose," came Margo's voice from his side as he drove, "this must be part of the plan we're working for?"

"I think it must."

"And what do you think of it now?" she asked bitterly.

"It sickens me."

"Does it? Wouldn't you have done it if you had to? You killed Joe Banks."

"Yes. And despite my misgivings, it hasn't troubled me seriously since. But Hever was a White Star. What kind of beings could kill a man like that, destroy a mind like that, of any race, for any reason?"

She could hear that he meant what he said. "I'm sorry," she told him. "Whatever happens, we're together."

At the door of her flat she grasped his arm. "Don't go," she said. He kissed her lightly, but freed himself.

He had only told her part of how he felt. The murder of Hever frightened him. What else was being done that he didn't know about? Who else had to die? How could he succeed when he didn't know what he was trying to do, when others, apparently, were working independently toward the unknown goal?

He doubted himself and his task, and he wanted to know more. He wanted to know enough for his own choice to be free.

chapter sixteen

RAIGMORE PASSED RAPIDLY THROUGH THE FINAL STAGES OF the Tests. The second-last was a test of responsibility, a Test which in effect decided whether a man was so fundamentally stable and good that he could rule the world, selflessly, if necessary. The Tests from beginning to end were based on a premise which so far had been sound—that the mind which was proved to be perfectly integrated was altruistic and just in the highest sense.

In his thesis on the Test system, the last Test of all, he tightened it so that never again could anyone like him pass through the Tests without the alien element showing; the Tests were that much nearer being perfect.

But that didn't affect the status of Eldin Raigmore, White Star.

book two

chapter one

THE BANK MANAGER WAS INCREDULOUS BUT VERY CIVIL. HE tried hard to conceal his incredulity, since what Raigmore said might possibly be true.

Raigmore didn't blame him for not believing it. There was no public announcement when a White Star was found. White Stars naturally kept in the background as much as they could, and so far no one who would gossip about Raigmore's new status knew it. As far as the bank manager was concerned, the only White Star about Raigmore's age in existence was Alison Hever. After this, however, it would soon be known everywhere that there was another, Eldin Raigmore. Things like that couldn't stay private for long.

"Check with the Tests Depot," Raigmore suggested. The manager would naturally do that anyway, but it saved him embarrassment if the suggestion came from Raigmore.

"This is a pure formality, of course," said the manager apologetically, perhaps beginning to believe that Raigmore's story was true.

It took only a few minutes to establish that there was a

new White Star, and that Raigmore was he. The manager's reserve vanished completely.

"There's no limit," he said. "Your bond is enough, Mr. Raigmore."

It was rare for White Stars to borrow money. They could easily make it if they happened to want it. A few minutes of a White Star's time were worth the huge sums that were generally paid for them. When a big, disturbing problem held up a firm, an industry or a government, White Stars could always see what often stumped the giant calculating machines used in industry these days—not the answer, necessarily, but how to get it.

Sometimes, however, when a White Star wanted money quickly, he would borrow it from a bank as Raigmore was doing. The transaction was rather different from such transactions before the Tests. The banks knew that a White Star would repay the loan, automatically, whenever he could. Even if he died, the other White Stars would pay the debt to protect their privileges and from a sense of justice. There was a certain clannishness among all Test groups, even at the top.

Raigmore had a mischievous impulse to name some astronomical figure, to see what happened. But he gave the modest figure he had decided on. He could have borrowed it from Margo, and he would have done so if his purpose had been anything else.

The manager, who had been so doubtful such a short time since, begged him to take more. Raigmore remarked reasonably, however, that there was no point in paying interest on more than he needed.

He had now announced himself, he thought as he left the bank. Within a day or two everyone in the solar system would know there was a new White Star. It was easy to guess how it would happen. In a few hours all Millo would know; in a day or two every newspaper on Earth would find some excuse for mentioning his name. It was contrary to journalistic etiquette for them to announce baldly that Eldin Raigmore had passed out as a White Star at Millo; but it was quite in order for them to say, with the timeless cunning of newspapermen, that Eldin Raigmore, White Star, had been seen at the new play, or at a football game, or anywhere else. The smarter newsmen would find some anecdote or item of news concerning him that was worth printing in itself, and was therefore a flawless excuse for giving his name and Test rank.

He went straight to the offices of a steamship company and bought two tickets for a private cruise. Travel by sea now was almost all for pleasure. Air services, both passenger and freight, were so numerous, competitive and fast that trade by sea had dropped to a trickle. The fight for supremacy was now between planed aircraft and rockets. The rockets were winning as far as freight was concerned, but people still persisted in regarding winged aircraft as safer for personal travel.

The girl at the glass and chromium desk noticed he wore no badge, and unconsciously straightened, patted her hair into place and became brisker and more deferent. "Do you wish to travel incognito, sir?" she asked.

"If possible. Is it?"

"We must know who you are, sir, but it's in order for

anyone who need not wear a badge to give a pseudonym. It's a private cruise, you see."

"Logical enough," Raigmore commented. A private cruise was merely one on which no badges need be worn— a pleasure cruise, in fact, where a certain amount of informality was permissible, like a private party. People could meet and mingle without the self-consciousness of rank, as they could on other informal occasions. It was therefore logical, as Raigmore said, that the top groups, whose names might be known, should be permitted to masquerade like everyone else.

When Raigmore gave his own name the girl, naturally, didn't turn a hair. But when he mentioned Alison Hever, equally naturally she jumped and stared at him.

She recovered herself after a second or two. "Shall we send Miss Hever the ticket, sir?" she asked.

"Please do. I can take it no one will know we're aboard?"

"Unless someone recognizes you embarking, sir. We guarantee that there will be no leakage through us." She was still staring at him. Alison Hever, probably, was her ideal, her model. And if Raigmore was on such terms with Alison that he could invite her along on a pleasure cruise, he became automatically the most interesting male alive.

Raigmore visited Margo on his way back to his hotel. She tried to act casually, but she couldn't help lighting up when she opened the door of her flat and ushered him in.

Some people would get a great kick out of this attention, Raigmore thought. Only, perhaps unfortunately, none of them would be White Stars. If you enjoyed the feeling of power that this deference gave you, you weren't properly integrated and couldn't be a White Star.

"I'm going away on a cruise, Margo," he said.

She looked surprised. "On a cruise? Why?"

"I want to see the world."

Margo frowned. "You couldn't be running away, could you?"

"From what? I'm taking a rest, yes. This is an interlude, a relaxation—it's just filling in time. But why not? I've done everything I can do. Except marry Alison."

A shadow crossed Margo's face. "She's going with you, then?"

"I hope so. I didn't actually ask her."

"She'll go. Unless—it's hardly a week since her father was killed. . . ."

"That won't make any difference. Not to Alison."

At one time a girl who didn't go into mourning in such circumstances would have been regarded as callous. But fashions had changed; any kind of mourning now was considered unnecessary show. Wearing black and staying away from entertainments of any kind made no difference to the dead person. Grief was private—no one else felt it. It would be in bad taste now to declare by one's clothes and conduct that one was still suffering after someone's death.

Margo turned and looked out at the window so that he couldn't see her face. "Why are you marrying Alison?" she asked quietly. "Because you want to or because you think you ought to?"

"Both," said Raigmore. "At first it was all because I thought it was part of my job to do it if I could. Now, if

I discovered I was wrong and that I was forbidden to marry Alison . . ."

He paused, uncertain. "I'd still want to anyway," he said. "I think I still would unless it meant some sort of danger to Alison. Is that frank enough for you?"

"Yes," said Margo slowly, as if the word was dragged out of her. "How much does your job matter to you now?"

"I feel I must still do it, whatever it is."

She turned quickly. "Though Hever was murdered?"

"You know what I think of the murder of Hever. But it may have been necessary, all the same."

"Necessary!" Margo exclaimed vehemently. "Didn't you ask what kind of beings could kill a man like that, destroy a mind like that, of any race, for any reason? Have you had second thoughts, and decided it wasn't really so important after all?"

"I've had second thoughts," said Raigmore. "I haven't decided it really wasn't so important after all, but I've seen some of the reasons there could have been for it. Suppose Hever had been just about to do something, and the only way to stop him doing it was to kill him? Suppose he had learned about us? Suppose he was just going to learn about us? If either you or Hever had to die, who would it have been?"

Margo was silent for a long time. At last she said with quiet intensity: "Why weren't you and I born just ordinary people, knowing where we stood, without this shadow always behind us? We could have been happy—couldn't we?"

Perhaps the difference between Red and White Star was

that, while Margo wanted the circumstances to change themselves, Raigmore wanted to change them, and was quite confident of being able to do it if only he knew what they were. He shook his head.

"We'd have been quite different," he said. "Listen, Margo, I'm not saying this to hurt you. You only want me because like clings to like. Your problems are mine too. Because we both have to solve them you think we should solve them together. If this other thing was cleared away, I'd be nothing to you."

She turned away and began to prowl about the room restlessly, picking up things and laying them down again.

"Perhaps something will happen when I marry Alison," said Raigmore. "That may be the signal. But if nothing ever does happen, so much the better."

He turned to go. Margo darted across the room and caught his arm. "What am I to do?" she asked desperately.

"I can't tell you. Whatever you think you ought to do."

"Do you think you ought to go away and enjoy yourself?"

"No. I don't think I ought to do anything, just at the moment. So I'm free to do as I like."

When he was outside he stared for several minutes at the closed door, wondering if there was anything else he should have done or said. He wanted to help Margo. But at the same time he knew that she had to work out her own salvation. One of his reasons for going away was to give her a chance to do it.

There was another difference between him and Margo. He would always do what he regarded as his duty—naturally, without conflict. But Margo, more emotional, would always be torn between duty and desire. More emotional? No, she wasn't really. There were so many stages. A man who strangled his emotion was only half a man. A man who let emotion rule him absolutely was a beast. One had to achieve a balance.

He didn't give himself any credit for it, but he had at last achieved that balance. Everyone who was a White had. That was why Alison would probably come on this cruise, though it was such a short time since her father had been murdered.

When he had met Margo first, he had been torn by emotion, she comparatively stable. He had climbed past her; now she was doubtful and fearful and indecisive by contrast.

Alison rang him almost as soon as he reached his hotel.

"I've just been sent a ticket for a sea cruise," she said.

"That's funny," said Raigmore, "I've got one too."

"If I come, does that mean . . . ?"

"It doesn't have to mean anything."

"Where did you get the money?"

"Borrowed it."

"From Margo?"

"Now, Alison," said Raigmore gently, "would I borrow it from Margo?"

A pause. "I suppose not. I'll come."

chapter two

THE "LEVIATHAN" GLIDED SMOOTHLY BUT RAPIDLY OVER A
choppy sea that might have been glass for all the effect it
had on the liner's steady motion. It had crossed the equator
the day before, but it wasn't too hot on deck. The speed
of the ship's passage produced a cooling breeze.

Raigmore ambled along the deck, glancing casually at
the men in white ducks, small and tubby, the massive, sun-
frocked women, the thin men in trunks and spectacles, the
callipygous girls in shorts and sweaters, the children in sun
suits. They were a good-looking lot, but there would never
be a wholly attractive race of human beings. For standards
changed; the brunette in the red shorts, Raigmore reflected,
would probably have been a beauty two or three centuries
ago, but now she would merely be rated quite attractive.
The woman with the straw hat would have been a remark-
ably well-preserved matron of sixty only a century ago,
but now, because her waistline was thirty-three, she was
fat. The man in the white trunks was really a magnificent
specimen, but since his biceps and calves and thighs were
rather too obvious he would be regarded as lean and stringy.

Centuries of good feeding had produced a near-perfect
race. Malnutrition was almost unheard of. It was recognized
at last that it was much better to cure things before they
happened than after.

There was always an atmosphere of ease and freedom and relaxation when there were no badges about. Though it was agreed that the Tests in general were a good thing, one body of opinion held that people's ratings should be comparatively private, not branded on their brows, so to speak. But Raigmore believed, as most people did, that the present system was better. One didn't expect more from people than they were capable of. Half the misery of the world had come from misunderstanding of one kind or another which could be avoided when everyone wore a badge that indicated what could be expected of him. No one, now, had to do anything that was beyond him.

Nevertheless, it was pleasant for most people to go out for a while and mingle with others freely, without the label Average, Good, Very Good or Excellent. It was like changing out of stiff, uncomfortable clothes into old, friendly clothes, or from a heavy, formal suit into shorts on a hot day. It was like going out for a drink with friends after a tiring day. It could be relaxing from the strain of being a Yellow Circle—for it was a strain—and pretending, gleefully, to be just another Brown or Purple. Or it could be the game of looking wise and smiling at secret jokes and saying things one knew were clever and being taken for a Red instead of a Purple. That was always a great joke.

Also it was the time when strong people, handsome people, athletic people could find free, unalloyed appreciation of their physical gifts. The Brown who had a strong back could throw Reds and Oranges on the gymnasium mat. The Purple whose badminton was her only talent could conquer Oranges and Yellows and feel a glow of pride that in one thing, in a free, unrated community, she was right at the top. The beautiful White, like Alison, could for once be just a pretty girl instead of a being so high above the common herd that it was almost impertinence to say so.

And it was the time of romance, too, when the man who sat next to one might be a White Cross on vacation, the girl opposite a fairy princess—that is, about fifteen grades higher than oneself.

Raigmore liked the atmosphere. He had been in an atmosphere of strain, of urgency, of being under close scrutiny almost all his life on Earth. For once he could relax and look on and be interested.

He joined a girl in slacks and halter leaning on the rail. "Miss Hamilton, I presume?" he said.

Alison turned and smiled at him. "Oh, it's Mr. Baker," she said. "R. S. Baker, isn't it? What does the R stand for—Raigmore?"

"No, Robert. Call me Bob."

"And you can call me Alice. You have, anyway. Why did you pick Alice Hamilton?"

"In case you had your initials on anything. Are the dark glasses meant to hide Alison Hever?"

"They have, so far. I've been completely ignored, even by Mr. Baker. Isn't it rather unusual to invite a girl on a cruise and only speak to her for the first time thirty-six hours out?"

"Ignored?" said Raigmore indignantly, playing his part. "This is the first time I've been able to get you alone. How about the seven men who just left you?"

Alison waved them aside negligently. "They talked to me as a face, not a White. Still, I'm glad to see you counted them."

"As a face?" repeated Raigmore, and stepped back to look properly at her. "Yes, that's true," he admitted. "You have a face."

His gaze, however, had made it clear that he didn't think it was her face the seven men had noticed. Alison's beauty was greater than the sum of its parts. She had the model's gift of making what she happened to be wearing seem the only possible dress for her, the outfit she would always look best in. Her white slacks concealed her long, smooth legs, but that was no loss. They made up for it by setting off the graceful lines of waist, hips and stomach. Revealing the midriff was risky, though so many girls did it, but in Alison's case the gamble came off. It was slim enough, and neat enough, and soft enough to show that most girls should hide that part of their bodies and be glad they had the chance. Her breasts, neatly clad in green chiffon, were pert but not unduly emphatic, and looking at them, one realized abruptly that most of the girls on the deck were too naked and too big-breasted.

Her face—yes, they might have been looking at her face after all. For if Alison had had an ugly body and that face, she would have been beautiful. The sunglasses hid her blue eyes, but they didn't obscure the delicate line of cheek-bone, the sparkling teeth, the small, straight nose and the well-shaped forehead. And from a distance the first thing to be noted would be her gleaming dark hair. She made blondes look cheap.

Raigmore took all this as his subject. "You're lovely, Alison, even with the dark glasses. I never saw anything lovelier."

"I thought we were supposed to be above that sort of thing," she said with a grin.

"So we are—supposed to be, I mean. From the Browns' point of view we're above just about everything. Well, are we?"

"Of course not. But I'm not used to being told I'm lovely, except by the most casual acquaintances. Those seven, for example. And that's quite different."

"Yes, people who know you better tell you what a wonderful mind you have. Isn't that exciting?"

She laughed. "No, but it's usual. This . . ."

"I see. Woman first, White Star second. You want me to tell you all about it. Why you're lovely, how lovely you are . . ."

She protested, but he told her. She resigned herself to being told how beautiful she was, and apparently managed to enjoy it.

"You're a puzzle, Bob," she said. "You've changed a lot. I'm sure it's you that's changed, not me."

"Yes, people change," Raigmore admitted. A few weeks earlier when someone said anything like that he would have been tensed, alerted by the remark, and would have tried to quiet the suspicions of the person who had made it. Now he realized there weren't really any suspicions, only curiosity and interest. "How did you feel about becoming a White Star, Alice?"

"A little surprised, that's all. I knew my father was much

wiser and bigger in every way than I was." She was able to talk quite easily, already, about her father. But Raigmore guessed there was something in her eyes which the sunglasses hid. "I didn't think I was in the same class as he. I'm not really—White Star is the top, open end. Not between A and B, like the White Crosses, but B plus. B plus one or B plus a thousand. He was further along than I am."

"Were the Tests the same for you as for me?"

"Pretty much."

"Who was your boy friend?"

Alison smiled mockingly. "Jealous? That was before I knew you existed."

Before I did exist, Raigmore thought. Before May 23.

"He was my first beau, Jack Crossman. A Red Circle. I thought I was in love with him. But when I shot past him in the Tests he dropped me like a hot brick."

Being a Red Circle, he would. Men of the lower Red groups seldom married women who were higher. The Reds were for the most part egotistical—not markedly so, but too much the egotist to marry women rated higher than themselves. Quite a lot of the famous egotists of the past would have been Reds.

"There's still a twinge, isn't there?" he said sympathetically.

She laughed a little awkwardly, for her. "I did feel it was unjust, somehow," she admitted. "I couldn't help climbing higher in the Tests. And it gets lonely. There are a lot of Jack Crossmans."

"I know," he said. He didn't really, but he could imagine it. People who felt inferior had a lot of different things they could do about it. Some would try to possess the thing to which they felt inferior, some would try to destroy it, and others would have nothing to do with it. Alison, young, beautiful, desirable and a White Star, must have encountered them all. The Jack Crossmans, who would have as little to do with her as possible; the men who would dislike her, vex her and hinder her as much as they could; and the men who would try to own her to prove they were better than she was. She must have thought, at first, that he was one of that class.

Cut out all those, cut out the Blacks and Grays, Browns and Purples, who could hardly be companions for a White, and there wasn't much left. Raigmore and Alison, thinking the same thing, knew then that they were going to marry. Raigmore was probably the only White Star Alison would ever have the chance to marry—the others were already married, or old, or in some other way disqualified. And if she waited for another White Star to emerge from the Tests she might wait the rest of her life. Alison was never likely to be quite as happy with any Yellow or lower White as with a White Star.

"It's different for men," she said, following out the thought. "Men can marry women ten grades below them and live quite happily. You could marry Margo."

"But I won't. How about it, Alice—do you want to stop being lonely?"

"Yes," she said, "but don't ask me yet. Wait till it comes naturally."

She turned and walked along the deck. Raigmore fell in at her side. "Let's go back to why you've changed," she said. "You think the Tests did it?"

"Not entirely, of course. But think of it this way. As a Black I was a misfit. I'd always been a misfit, always wrong, always different from everybody else. You grew up among Whites and Yellows—I didn't. I was on the defensive, yet aggressive. I thought I was better than the people round me, but was always afraid I wasn't. Do you see?"

"Yes, I see," said Alison. "I never thought of it like that. There couldn't be any greater misfit than a White Star among Blacks and Grays and Browns."

She pressed his arm warmly, feeling she understood him better. Raigmore was a little ashamed of himself.

chapter three

THEY GREW INTO EACH OTHER'S LIFE IN THE NEXT FEW DAYS, knowing it was for keeps. Superficially they were like most of the other young couples on board. They played games, swam in the ship's swimming pools, danced in the ballroom, sun-bathed on deck. But they were probing deeper into each other's characters, learning more than any of the other couples.

Raigmore had thought it would be a slow, wonderful business, getting to know Alison, and he had been right.

Sometimes the wideness of her interests startled him. His own interests were expanding rapidly, but they had a long way to go to catch up with hers.

She was delighted by a TV concert given by the Vienna

Philharmonic Orchestra, relayed from Austria, and enjoyed a jam session by members of the ship's band. One of the few times Raigmore heard her say anything cynical was when he quoted a statement that people who liked all kinds of music had neither taste nor understanding. "That was said," she observed, "by someone who thought he had taste and understanding, but didn't get much out of life."

She didn't do everything well. She played card games only moderately, though she enjoyed them, because her main interest was always in finding out things, not in winning. She found out about the other players, about how they played and thought, and if she could do that they could win for all she cared. When Raigmore was concentrating on exactly where the fifty-two cards were and how he could do what should not, on the cards, be possible, she would be working out, from Mrs. Parker's cosmopolitan accent, the cities of the world in which she had lived.

Alison played a good game of tennis, but again winning didn't matter. She adjusted her style of play so that it would be a good match, and if the other girl was trying hard Alison generally let her win. Once when Alison and Raigmore had been playing against a rather obnoxious couple and lost narrowly, Raigmore found himself remarking with some heat that the Tomlinsons would be better taken down a peg or two instead of being allowed to think they were the better pair. Alison smiled and said: "Let them. It's the only thing they can do. We have a lot of other things."

She spent a good deal of time with the children in the nursery. On the ship, as in other places, many parents left their offspring in the kindergarten to be out of the way while they enjoyed themselves unencumbered. Alison became more popular than their parents with some of the children, which often had a good effect. Quite a few couples, after hearing how marvelous Alice Hamilton was, devoted more attention to their children.

Alison wasn't sentimental or idealistic about children—she never said, "Isn't he a little dear," or gave any indication of thinking that children were angels. "They're little criminals," she said cheerfully, "or they would be if they had enough power. They should be taught how to handle power, in small doses, and shown that power means responsibility."

Raigmore liked to watch her with the children, but was slow to enter into her play with them. "I like them all right," he said, "but I don't understand them."

"Neither do I," said Alison. "Nobody does. Certainly not the child psychologists. They're still doing what they've been doing for hundreds of years—working out charts, testing, classifying, theorizing. Anything but understanding."

"What are children then—mysteries?"

"Exactly. Little mysteries. Interesting little mysteries."

After that Raigmore began to join in the play.

No one identified Alison and Raigmore. Raigmore guessed it was because when people looked at Alice Hamilton now and noticed how closely she resembled Alison Hever, they were already quite certain that she couldn't be Alison Hever because she didn't behave at all like a White Star. Not, at any rate, as they believed a White Star would behave.

They didn't keep to themselves. Alison talked and danced

with quite a lot of other men, and once told Raigmore he'd better hurry up and propose, because she had had two proposals already. But for Alison this was nothing new. She had never been lonely in the social sense. There had always been plenty of people about her, people who were deferent, admiring, envious—people whose very presence showed her how alone she was. They were so conscious of the gap between her and them, whether they affirmed it or denied it, that she was kept conscious of it too. There were always so many things that she could share with so few people. That had been Alison's loneliness.

To Raigmore, however, the easy camaraderie of the ship was new and revealing. He had never had anything to do with crowds. He had never been in a gay, pleasure-bent company in which introductions were unnecessary, in which any two people finding themselves together for a moment would talk without reserve. He knew this fleeting contact was generally shallow and of little significance, but he found also that it needn't be shallow. He made many acquaintances whom he would be glad to see again anywhere, any time.

Before he went on board the *Leviathan* he had known, altogether, about twenty people. After a few days on the ship he knew a hundred, then two hundred. He discovered the pleasure of talking with someone about other people, agreeing and disagreeing about them. He discovered how pleasant it was to find common ground with someone he'd just met. He found out a lot of things which most people his age had been taking for granted for most of their lives.

He developed an easy, flippant way of talking based on

Fred Salter's. He knew it wasn't the ultimate answer, but he found it served very well for the time being. Gradually, he believed, his own personality would emerge from under that pattern.

He was surprised, pleased and a little shocked to find how quickly women took to him. He had never thought of himself as attractive, but whenever Alison wasn't around he was liable to find himself in the company of some pretty girl or other, and almost before he knew her first name a mild flirtation would be going on.

Fran, one of the first, was typical. A trim figure in white nylon shorts, a vivid scarlet blouse and a peaked cap, she walked with the grace of a model and knew it. She bumped into Raigmore without much pretense that it was an accident and clutched at him to save herself from falling.

"You're Bob, aren't you?" she said, her arms round his neck. "I'm Fran."

Rather startled, Raigmore found himself and Fran in one deck chair less than a minute later. He made a few ineffectual attempts to convince Fran that she would be much more comfortable in a chair of her own, feeling as he did so that a White Star ought surely to be capable of handling the situation better. It wasn't that he minded Fran sitting on his knee, half smothering him with golden hair and brown arms—that was quite pleasant in a disturbing sort of way. But he was uneasily conscious that Alison might think unfortunate things for her to think if she happened to come past just then.

It was only when he realized that Fran was just playing, a happy child having fun with her capacity for putting up male temperature, that he began to feel in control of the situation again. He kissed her and enjoyed it. She seemed to have no objections either. He gained a little valuable experience in what to do with a girl sitting on his knee, then got up with Fran in his arms and put her down in the deck chair.

"Glad to have met you, Fran," he said, "but I've got a date with my fiancée now. Cheerio."

It was astonishing how quickly girls learned he was harmless. Very soon there were a lot of Frans. One after another they threw themselves at his head, knowing he would catch them and set them gently on their feet. Not all of them wanted that, of course.

Presently, instead of hoping Alison wouldn't find him with the Fran of the moment, he made sure she did. Almost at once this had the desired effect.

"All right," said Alison, after seeing him dance a kiss waltz with a girl who was co-operating enthusiastically, "you win. I have to stop that somehow. I wouldn't like you to think I'm jealous—but all the same, I'd quite gladly tear that girl's hair out by the roots."

"What do I win?" Raigmore asked blandly.

"Me," said Alison simply.

But she wouldn't let him kiss her, to seal it, as he said. "Recent events," she said darkly, "are still too fresh in my mind. Come on, let's dance."

So Raigmore never did actually propose. In a business-like way they arranged for the captain to marry them, took a vacant bridal suite for the rest of the cruise after the ceremony, and carried on exactly as before. There was no need to be sentimental about it, Alison said. It was a business contract, each agreeing it was a good thing.

Raigmore's recent experience had given him a few other ideas, but he didn't insist on them. It seemed to him that, short of living in sin, they might quite reasonably begin the business of getting used to each other before they suddenly found themselves husband and wife. He wondered what it would be like, for example, to share a deck chair with Alison instead of Fran, or sit alone with her in the moonlight instead of dancing decorously in the ballroom, or at least kiss her good night. He thought that when he was waiting in or around Alison's cabin for her to get ready she might be a little less strict in her views of what was decent—there were a lot of little things.

Alison, however, had always had to be careful that she didn't give the wrong impression, and her decorum stuck. She wasn't unduly strict in her manner or modest in her dress, but she was always very correct. And when Raigmore hinted that it was hardly necessary to be quite so correct with him now, she laughed but kept him at arms' length.

"What would the Browns say?" she asked.

"I don't give a damn," he admitted.

"But I do. If the Browns aren't to be promiscuous, the Whites mustn't be promiscuous. See?"

So Raigmore shrugged and left it at that.

chapter four

RAIGMORE GOT THE OPPORTUNITY TO SAY "I TOLD YOU SO." Presently he and Alison found themselves, rather taken aback, actually being married.

The captain and a few of his officers and the witnesses had to know who Alice and Bob actually were, but there was no need for anyone else to know. Everyone knew Bob and Alice were getting married, but that was all they knew.

After the brief ceremony Raigmore and Alison, still rather surprised about it all, wandered in the direction of their new suite. Suddenly Raigmore stopped dead.

A man coming along the corridor in the opposite direction changed his mind when he saw them and hurried back the way he had come. If he hadn't turned, Raigmore wouldn't have noticed him at all.

The man was Bill Carter.

Raigmore was inexplicably, unreasonably angry. He wanted to go after Carter and strike him down. He saw some of the reasons for his anger, though the force behind it remained inexplicable. He had told the man to stop following him around, and here he was, a grim reminder of things Raigmore wanted to forget, just when he had all but succeeded in forgetting them. He resented the time it had happened, too. All his attention should be for Alison—if he had seen Carter earlier or later it might have been interesting, something to think about. But now Carter was an intrusion, a reminder that he was *different* when, of all times, he didn't want to be reminded that he was anything but an ordinary human being.

Alison misinterpreted his sudden halt. She hadn't noticed Carter. She stopped too and smiled wryly at Raigmore.

"You were absolutely right, of course," she said.

Raigmore dragged his attention back from Carter as much as he could. "Nervous?" he asked sympathetically.

"A little. I hadn't realized we'd hardly touched each other. I mean, we've danced, but I must have danced at one time or another with more than a thousand men. I haven't even kissed you. And now . . ."

Raigmore smiled. "What does it matter?"

"It does matter. You know it does. We should have been ready for this—I mean, I should. A few minutes ago I was Alison Hever, and now suddenly I'm Alison Raigmore. And I'm not ready to be Alison Raigmore yet."

Raigmore was still smiling. "Tell you what," he said. "You know that seat on F deck at the stern where no one ever sits because of the spray?"

She nodded.

"I don't mind a little spray, do you?"

Alison laughed. "No, not in a good cause."

"Suppose you think it over for half an hour or so, get used to the idea of being Alison Raigmore, and come along and meet me there?"

"In a raincoat?"

"If you like. I won't complain."

She considered it for a moment. "You are understanding,

Eldin," she said a little awkwardly. "I think you're big in the way my father was big. You never blame anyone for anything. You just take things as they are and shrug your shoulders."

"I wish you were right," murmured Raigmore. "You called me Eldin. Have we stopped being Bob and Alice?"

"It's a queer name. I have to get used to using it." She paused, trying to think of something else to say, then turned abruptly and went along the corridor.

That left Raigmore free to go after Carter.

He guessed Carter would be on board under his own name. It was all very well for Whites to travel under pseudonyms, but Blacks had few privileges. A lot of trifling things were offenses for Blacks and no one else. It wasn't that Blacks were hounded and persecuted and irritated as much as possible in scores of petty ways—it was part of the Tests system that it should be to everyone's advantage to take the Tests and have a rating. If Blacks had the same privileges as everyone else there would be no motive, for many people, to become rated at all.

It would be a fairly serious offense for a Black to pretend to be someone else, even in cases like this. There was always the consideration that any Black could be a criminal, while it was most unlikely that anyone else was, except Grays.

Raigmore found the cabin number of Bill Carter and went straight to it. He hesitated outside the door, wondering what he was going to say. He could reach no conclusion, however. It all depended on what Carter had to say. He knocked boldly and went in.

Carter was alone, apparently waiting for him.

"I want an explanation, Carter," said Raigmore coldly.

Carter was acting better than the last time he had seen him. He had acquired manners, gestures, expressions. They still didn't seem to mean much, but Raigmore knew that that might be a purely subjective conclusion.

"Of what, Mr. Raigmore?" Carter asked.

"Have you told anyone I'm Raigmore?"

"Of course not."

Raigmore was going to ask why not, but that was a side issue. "You told me you were under my orders. I didn't order you to come on this cruise. Where did you get the money, anyway?"

Carter ignored the last question. "I have to look after you," he said.

Raigmore shook his head impatiently. "That won't do. I'm in no danger here that I know of. If you do, I'd like to know what it is."

Carter was silent.

"What are you doing here?" Raigmore insisted.

Carter shook his head.

"You know more than I do," Raigmore said. "You must. I'm in earnest, Carter—I must know everything there is to know."

"It wouldn't interest you."

"I'm telling you it does interest me. What you know may be of no actual use to me, but I want it anyway."

Carter looked back at him steadily, but didn't open his mouth. Raigmore had seldom been angry, but he found himself furious now. Perhaps it was because he felt insecure with Carter, because Carter had information that might be vital, information that was denied Raigmore. Raigmore's anger was partly the annoyance of a figurehead commander who finds suddenly that others technically below him, his assumed inferiors, have orders that override his. But Raigmore was also angry because Carter represented his weak spot. He was safe among the teeming millions of Earth, but he was vulnerable to Carter.

He wanted to shake the truth out of Carter, but he knew without trying it that it would be a waste of time. Carter and Peach were two of a kind. Either of them would die on the rack silent—they would be tortured to death before they would say anything they didn't mean to say. Margo, now—probably Margo would break down if the ordeal was great enough. Perhaps in that weakness lay the essential humanity of Margo.

No, Raigmore knew instinctively that if he was to get anything out of Carter he would have to show good reason. He fought down his anger. Anger implied failure, present, past or future. And Raigmore meant to succeed, if he had to work on Carter till they were both reeling with fatigue.

"Listen, Carter," he said more quietly. "I'm not going to tell you anything because I don't trust you. You haven't given me any reason to trust you. I might have a reason now that made it absolutely imperative that I get from you anything you know—but I wouldn't tell you it. Do you see that?"

"Is there such a reason?"

"Obviously I wouldn't tell you. You believe in reasons, don't you, Carter?"

"Doesn't everyone?"

"Yes, but I think you do particularly. Human beings often act on things you wouldn't call reasons. You know that, don't you?"

He hadn't finished that line, but he saw it wasn't leading anywhere with Carter. He tried again.

"All right, then, I'll give you a reason. A good reason." He paused to make sure he meant what he was going to say, and found he did. "If you don't, I'm going to tell Alison everything *I* know."

"You must not," said Carter quickly.

"No?" Raigmore inquired. He knew he was on the right track at last. "Tell me why, then."

"You wouldn't do it. You wouldn't betray . . ."

"Betray what, Carter? How can I betray a thing when I don't know what it is? All I can do is tell Alison a few things I know, and add a few more things that I've guessed. I can do that, and I will."

He waited. Carter's expression didn't change, but he was obviously working the whole thing out, calculating whether Raigmore would do as he said, what he could tell Raigmore and how much it mattered if he did.

He came to decision. "I'll tell you," he said. "But you must realize it's nothing. Would our race leave valuable information around to be picked up?"

"Ah," said Raigmore softly. "Our race. What is our race?"

"I don't know, except that it isn't this one."

"Another human race?"

"I don't know. I suppose it must be."

"Why do you suppose that?"

"We're human . . . but you know as much about that as I do. More, probably."

Raigmore sighed. He believed Carter when he said he didn't know what race they belonged to. Clearly Carter didn't think that point of much importance.

"Go on," he said.

"Our people will come," said Carter, "and we have to prepare for them."

"Why?"

It was another question that had no meaning for Carter. "They will come," he repeated, as if that explained everything.

"From where?"

"They will come. From somewhere."

Raigmore felt helpless. "From space?" he asked.

"I suppose so. If you think so, probably."

"Why? Am I supposed to know more than you?"

"You once did."

At last Carter had said something. Those three words didn't mean that Raigmore simply had to think and he would remember everything—he had already tried all the variations on that he could think of. But they did mean that Raigmore, after all, was more important than Carter. His part mattered more. And therefore he was more in control of the situation.

"Our people will come," said Raigmore patiently. "And I once knew all about it. Am I supposed to know this now?"

"No. You're supposed to know nothing."

"What else do you know?"

"That I must say close to you whatever you do. I must protect you."

"Against whom?"

"I don't know."

For twenty minutes or so Raigmore put all the questions he could think of, phrasing them differently in the hope that Carter might be able to answer some of them or some parts of them. But he didn't get anything else until:

"Who will benefit when our people come?" Raigmore asked. "What will they do?"

He had asked questions very like this before and received no answer. Carter still seemed to be co-operating. He answered all he could, and Raigmore was prepared to believe that when he said he didn't know it was true.

This time apparently the mention of the word "benefit" aroused something in Carter.

"They will come to benefit Earth," he said. "They will come to give, not to take."

Raigmore stared at him. Carter didn't seem at all interested in this either. The purpose of the invasion, or influx, or whatever it was mattered no more to him than when it would be. Raigmore had tried to pin him down to a time—more than a week, less than a year, more than fifty years—without success. Carter didn't know and didn't care. They would come.

Now this. *They will come to benefit Earth. They will come to give, not to take.*

Raigmore worked on this till the words ceased to have any meaning. Was Carter supposed to tell him that?

No.

Was he supposed to tell anyone that?

No.

Was there anything he could add to it?

No.

Was it in those words?

No. It wasn't in any words.

Raigmore got nothing more. Carter was squeezed dry. But it was a crumb of comfort. Carter really believed that this other race, to which he, Raigmore, Fenton, Peach and Margo belonged, was coming to help Earth. *To give, not to take.* Carter himself was indifferent to Earth, as to almost everything else. He wouldn't lie. It was of no consequence to him, but it was a fact—the coming of the other race was going to be a great thing for Earth. He couldn't understand why Raigmore insisted on it, asking the same question fifty different ways.

"Very well," said Raigmore at last. "Listen, Carter. I'm going to be with Alison from now on. Remember she's a White Star. You're not. Frankly, I doubt if you'd be higher than Purple. White Stars are not only clever, they're attentive, observant and efficient. If you go on trailing after me as you've been doing, I may not see you, but sooner or later she will. When she does she'll want to know why you're trailing me, and who you are, and a lot of other awkward things. So I think you'd better leave me entirely alone—don't you?"

"If you're going to make things difficult for me," said Carter, "I can no longer protect you."

He showed no resentment, as before. He saw that what

Raigmore said was true. There was no point, apparently, in resenting facts.

"Good," said Raigmore. He left the cabin, hoping he would never see Carter again.

chapter five

RAIGMORE LEANED ON THE RAIL, THINKING. WHAT HE wanted to do was tell Alison everything, anyway. He had given Carter no promise. But that was out of the question. Telling a whole story was possible, but giving her the few fragments he possessed would serve no useful purpose. She would believe him, no doubt; if believing such a story needed imagination and openness of mind, she had both. But the result would only be, at best, that she would be as puzzled as he was. No, it wasn't a practical proposition, trying to turn her into an ally or at least an interested onlooker.

He didn't think Carter would trouble him again. One of the big puzzles about the whole business was the immense difference in the members of his party. On the one hand, Carter and Peach; on the other, Margo and himself. It almost made him think there must be two separate groups pretending to work together. Yet Peach had done her job when he called on her, and he had no doubt that Carter, if he had been needed, would have been just as obedient and efficient.

He thought he could see why what Carter had to say had been so vague and stilted. Carter, though not brilliant, couldn't be a fool. It hadn't been mere lack of intelligence that had made him speak so vaguely. He was trying to put into words a knowledge that was not in words—an almost incomprehensible concept from the unremembered world. But why had Carter been left with a little more knowledge than Raigmore?

When Carter said "they will come" he must, Raigmore decided, have meant invasion from space. Nothing else made sense.

No other intelligent life had been found in the solar system. But intelligence was only a matter of degree. Plants had been found, and plants were intelligent; plants would be clever if there weren't so many cleverer organisms about. Somewhere there might exist creatures who were at least as intelligent as men.

If such creatures came to Earth could they benefit the humans? Undoubtedly they could. There were so many benefits that such a race might have to offer Earth that Raigmore left that line of speculation after a glance at some of them—immortality, trade, new sciences, the way to the stars.

Whether such benefits were likely from a meeting of the worlds was another matter. They were certainly possible.

Raigmore left it there. Seeing Carter and making him say what he knew hadn't really altered the situation much. He was still waiting. He was still resting, knowing nothing further he was supposed to do.

"I thought you weren't coming," said Alison in a small voice.

Surreptitiously he glanced at his watch. He was surprised to find it was nearly three hours since he had parted with Alison. She must have spent most of that time waiting there on F deck, for the spray, which was very thin and fine, had starred her hair and water glistened on her arms and legs. It was so warm, however, that the spray was no discomfort. She hadn't put on the raincoat she had threatened.

Raigmore took her gently in his arms and sensed to his astonishment that she was very near to tears. Could a White Star cry because someone was a couple of hours late? Apparently she could, if she was a woman and a bride of only an hour or two.

"Darling," he said into her hair. It was the first time he had used the word. "What did you think I was doing, marrying someone else?"

It was the right note. She was caught between laughing and crying, and the laughing won.

Presently she said: "It's quite easy and natural after all, isn't it? I just fit in your arms as if I'd always been there."

"You should have been," said Raigmore. "We've wasted twenty-three years."

Alison chuckled. When she spoke quietly her voice dropped much lower. "That's not serious," she murmured. "Do you know that on present expectation of life we have fully a hundred years left?"

"I don't guarantee to love you after you're a hundred."

"Don't you? Come to think of it, you never guaranteed

to love me at all. Isn't this a marriage of convenience?"

Raigmore kissed her lightly. "Must marriages of love be inconvenient?" he asked.

"You just kissed me."

"I know."

"But that was the first."

"Let's erect a monument to it. An oak tree, growing through the deck, with crossed hearts and 'Eldin loves Alison' carved on it." He kissed her again. "Now it's hardly worth it. It's no longer unique."

Alison sighed contentedly. "You talk a nice line of nonsense," she said.

"That's why Sally Morris made me a White Star. She liked my line."

"More important, darling—did you like hers? Tell me about all the girls you've ever loved."

"Only two."

"Two?"

"Alison Hever and Alice Hamilton."

"That's a lie, but I like it."

"It's the truth," Raigmore protested.

"You do this too well."

"Natural talent and due consideration. I made up my mind a long time ago that if I ever fell in love it would be with a woman."

"Just a woman? What a letdown. I thought for a moment you were going to tell me I was beautiful."

"Again?"

"The last time was weeks ago."

"But you're not used to it. It embarrasses you."

"I didn't run away screaming the last time."

"All right. I'll risk it."

When he had finished, Alison said breathlessly: "All that can't be true. You're making it up."

"Yes," Raigmore admitted, "I made it up."

They were still there when the sun set.

"Eldin," said Alison reluctantly, "it may be unromantic of me, but I'm getting hungry."

"Unromantic?" Raigmore exclaimed. "It's sacrilegious. Haven't I told you I love you?"

"Yes, I know," said Alison penitently, "but I'm still hungry. My stomach's touching my backbone."

"So it is. But then, it always does. So it doesn't mean anything. You're not hungry at all, Alison." He settled down comfortably again.

"We're both wet through, and it's getting colder. We must go and change."

Raigmore sighed and got up stiffly. "She loves me not."

They made their way to their suite and looked round it. Neither of them had been in it before.

"I think the ballroom is bigger," said Raigmore, surveying the lounge critically.

Alison laughed suddenly, helplessly. "I never thought you'd be like this, Eldin," she said.

"I'm not really," he told her soberly. "But there are times when if you didn't make a joke of things it would be hard to find anything to say. And we don't know each other well enough yet not to say anything, do we?"

"I think we do now," said Alison quietly.

Raigmore didn't see Carter again on the ship. The month of the cruise that remained was pure happiness. He refused to look beyond it.

Raigmore and Alison had notified the authorities of their marriage. They had also sent radiograms to Gloria, Salter and Margo. The replies came the same day.

Gloria's radiogram said: "Congratulations. You've both done very well for yourselves."

Margo's said: "I wish you every happiness," and left it at that.

Fred's read: "You could have knocked me down with a twenty-ton truck when I got your wire. Raigmore is crazy. Alison is crazier. I assume it only happened because Raigmore got Alison into trouble, but even so, don't you know there are homes for unmarried mothers? I can't reasonably wish you happiness, so I'll just wish you both modified misery."

"Fred doesn't mention Margo, or Margo Fred," Raigmore mused as they read the radiograms.

"Naturally not, when they're congratulating us," said Alison. "They don't say whether it's raining in Millo either."

But Raigmore wondered. It was by no means necessary for Margo to marry Salter, or anyone else for that matter, but it was necessary for her to find some anchor in this world.

Just at the end of the cruise, in the last few days, it leaked out that Bob and Alice were not just Bob and Alice. A radio newscast from New York stated, rather late, that Alison Hever had married Eldin Raigmore, White Star, at sea. It was then easy enough to work out that Bob and Alice must be these two, though no ship was mentioned.

Raigmore and Alison became fervently glad that the truth about them hadn't been known before. When Raigmore appeared on deck for the first time after the news item, still hoping they hadn't been identified, he was mobbed. The lack of order and restrictions on board the ship, previously so pleasant, now made it positively dangerous to go on deck at all. The crowd meant no harm, but Raigmore had to fight his way back to the suite, minus his shirt and most of his trousers, which had been claimed by souvenir hunters.

Alison was amused. He didn't know how to handle a mob like that, she said. It wasn't his fault—he hadn't had practice. But she'd been used to it all her life. So she started out for the nursery that afternoon as usual.

There was a wild rush when she appeared on deck, but at first nothing happened except that what seemed like five thousand people with big cameras, small cameras, cine cameras and stereo cameras were trying to take pictures of her. Very soon, however, the press of people behind forced the photographers forward, and Alison found one camera digging into her ribs and another in her back.

Half an hour later she got back to the suite and Raigmore helped her to close the door. She was hot and breathless, her hair over one eye. Nothing remained of her frock and only rags of anything else. Scraps of cloth would be carefully preserved in notebooks by scores of souvenir hunters. She was bruised and scratched all over.

Raigmore assured himself that her injuries were slight

before he said: "Just as well you knew how to handle them, Alison."

She laughed breathlessly. "I didn't allow for the fact that there's no police and so many people in such a small space," she said. "Besides, they think that just being married makes me fair game, I suppose."

Raigmore started to clean her scratches. "I think the kids will have to get along without us from now on."

"Yes, we'd better stay put until the ship docks. This sort of thing isn't good for prestige."

"Not to mention clothes, a whole skin and peace of mind," Raigmore added.

They kept the door locked except when the steward appeared with their meals. The captain visited them and said apologetically there was nothing much he could do. He didn't have enough men to spare to detail a big enough bodyguard to be worth while.

Raigmore wasn't really sorry it had happened, though he was glad it hadn't come sooner. It was due warning of what would happen often in the future when people in the mass learned who he and Alison were.

"Anyway," he remarked cheerfully to the captain, as they showed him out, "I can think of worse things than being locked up for a day or two with Alison, can't you?"

From the captain's expression it seemed that he could.

book three

chapter one

RAIGMORE LAY IN THE SUNROOM AND LET HIS MIND TICK
over idly, out of gear. Soon Alison would join him there.
He was waiting, idle, content, nothing remaining to be
done that he could do. He was happy.

But he still wished that the shadow which lurked in the
back of his mind would disappear, or at least show its true
shape.

There had been no notable sequel to the murder of
Alison's father. Brolley had been discharged after therapy,
insignificant, harmless, an ordinary Brown using another
name, only slightly bewildered by the inconsistencies of his
life as he saw it. The case was closed on the discovery that
Brolley, when he was In Test, had been handled by an
inexperienced operator. A system is no more perfect than
the people who administer it, and it was assumed that the
operator in question hadn't followed up something which
would have been obvious to someone like Sally Morris. The
bottom limit for Test operators was moved one step higher,
and that was that.

Raigmore had another view, but he kept it to himself. Tests which weren't quite perfect right at the top, however infallible they might be in the middle, were also liable to be not quite perfect right at the bottom, and that was where Brolley was. He wasn't feeble-minded enough to be kept in an institution, but he certainly didn't have the intelligence to perform the Tests properly. The Tests had failed to find the dormant compulsion which had been planted deep in him because Brolley simply couldn't communicate.

Raigmore wondered what one could do with people like Brolley, ordinary humans like him. They were intelligent beings, after all—only they were so far behind everyone else that there was no niche in the world for them. The geniuses were one problem, the morons another. The Tests handled everyone else beautifully.

It was two weeks since Raigmore and Alison had returned from the cruise, and already Raigmore had repaid his debt to the bank. Alison concerned herself with personnel problems, which gave her something in common with Margo. But Margo had a job, and was expected to do it; Alison had none, only a hobby, an interest.

It could pay off, all the same. She had been given a job as soon as she came back, and had taken Raigmore along to help her to do it. An automobile factory in Detroit was going over to a new method of production. Their job was to regrade the whole personnel for the new conditions, find who could do what, who else would be needed, who had better be transferred to something else. They had worked hard for a week, learning and training, applying their unspecialized talent to the whole field. A mere psychologist could have done some of the job. A doctor could have done some of the rest. There would have been jobs for technicians, statisticians, engineers, electricians, executives and people with ordinary common sense. When Alison and Raigmore needed special knowledge they found someone who had it. For the rest they did everything themselves. And a job which would have taken an expensive special staff a month to do, with considerable loss in production, was handled smoothly in a week.

The Raigmores saved the firm concerned almost a million dollars. Their fee was fifty thousand. Everyone was satisfied.

Specialization had gone too far, then turned back. The stage had been reached where a man knew so much about so little that he often couldn't do his own job well, because other things would persist in crossing it. Often, in such cases, mere intelligence, comparatively uninstructed, was better. Intelligent people had a lot of information and knew where to get the rest.

White Stars were intelligent people *in excelsis*. They had no blank spots, or they couldn't be what they were. They tended to have more information, and more general information, at hand than anyone else. Without overspecializing, they were practically specialists in everything. So a White was always the best bet for any big, difficult job, if a White could be persuaded to do it. That wasn't always easy, even with an open checkbook.

White Stars were the free agents of the world. In a sense, everyone was free—certainly freer than they had been under any other system. But the Tests system carried its obligations. The Browns were free—within bounds of convention, law and their own limitations. The Purples and Reds, still within the law, were free to gratify anything but destructive whims. The Yellows and Oranges might almost be said to be above the law. They were expected to do certain things and behave in a certain widely bounded way. But it was the way they would naturally follow. It was rare for anyone to say to a member of either group "Thou shalt not . . ."

White Circles and Crosses were the rulers, rulers who seldom had to make a real decision and say "This is right" or "This is wrong," but rulers who ruled in explaining to the administrators. The real guiding hand of the world was the group authority of the lower Whites.

White Stars were—yes, it was the only way to put it— the gods of the race. In a sense they did nothing. They lived normal lives, or lives as near normal as they could, watching, waiting, sometimes suggesting, but usually merely keeping out of the way and letting others get on with the job, whatever the job was. The masses who had once thought Hever would be the next President had studied little history. It had seldom been necessary for any White Star to come out into the open. The President was a White Cross, as usual. He was a man named Harry Robertson, and if the lower ninety per cent of humanity cared to ask, they would be told that he was no more important than any other White Cross. But he was also no less.

Alison looked in, but stayed in the doorway. "Margo's coming over," she said.

"Why?" Raigmore asked bluntly.

"No particular reason. Well . . . there is a reason, of course. But wait till I change." She let the door swing shut behind her.

It might seem, Raigmore thought, that it couldn't be a perfect system in which the very best was wasted. For there was no co-ordinated effort to use the potential of the White Stars.

. What was kept in reserve, however, wasn't necessarily wasted. A world that functioned well didn't often have to go to the temple of the gods. In fact, it almost never happened. But the gods were there if they were needed, and they were such gods that they didn't waste in idleness. There was always something to do. One month it would be an automobile factory with a personnel problem. The next it would be an inexplicably high death rate somewhere. Another time it would be a ticklish political situation. Instead of being left to muddle through, on the old pattern, people could at least ask for White Star assistance. If it was really necessary, they generally got it.

White Stars could have been rich, but they weren't. The next time the Raigmores did a job, they would probably turn most of their fee in to reduce taxation. People who hoarded money were people who felt insecure.

Alison came in with supple grace and sank beside Raigmore on the foam-rubber flooring. She began: "Margo said——"

"Never mind Margo for a minute. Just because you're my wife you needn't stop kissing me when you come in."

"Fool," said Alison, but she kissed him.

"That's better. It's not that I enjoy it or anything like that, but I feel it's my duty."

Alison smiled. "I keep waiting for you to grow up."

"I have. It's just because I'm lying down that you don't notice it. I'm much bigger when I stand up. What was this about Margo?"

"Just the usual. She rang about something unimportant. Something she didn't need to ring me about. She seemed lonely. So I asked her to come over."

Raigmore frowned. Margo and he were bound together by a lot of different things. He liked her, and Alison liked her. But she didn't seem to be able to cut loose from him. He had hoped the break when he went on the cruise would make a difference, but it hadn't. She had heroically managed not to write to him, and she was obviously trying to remember that he was Alison's now, not hers—he had never been hers. She failed often, however, like an alcoholic trying not to drink and just having a little one, and then another little one.

Raigmore could understand it all right, and fortunately Alison could understand it too. It seemed natural to Alison that Margo should be in love with Raigmore.

Salter had got nowhere with Margo. There was only one thing really wrong with Salter from Margo's point of view, but that was insuperable. He wasn't Raigmore.

"You didn't make her fall in love with you, Eldin, did you?" asked Alison quietly.

"No. In a way it wouldn't be so bad if I had. I'd only have myself to blame, and I might be able to reverse the process. I wish she wouldn't discourage Fred so much. There's a little problem for you, White Star. Remove Margo's affections from me, where they're wasted and rather embarrassing, and set them on Fred, who would be highly delighted."

Alison took him seriously. "I'll see what I can do in a quiet way," she said. Whites generally did everything in a quiet way.

Alison might be able to do something where Raigmore couldn't. Margo admired her tremendously. Alison was all she wished she was herself.

They fell silent then, lying in the sun, and Raigmore tried to pursue his earlier line of thought. But something was wrong. It was nothing to do with Alison or Margo. It was just a hazy knowledge, a sudden hunch. He didn't examine it. Hunches weren't meant to be examined. You could use them, as you used a watch. A watch told you the time, and that was its sole purpose. If you began to examine it, to take it apart, it ceased to tell the time and became no longer a watch. It was only the parts of a watch.

Raigmore and Alison looked in perfect harmony in their silence, but presently Alison sensed the difference.

"What is it?" she asked. "Someone walking on your grave?"

"Nothing," he said. He knew at once that wouldn't do. "Well, there is something. Alison, don't you ever have hunches?"

"I used to," she said. "But some of them were wrong. I decided they were too risky. I stopped acting on them. So they stopped coming."

"I think you were wrong," he said. "You shouldn't have stopped acting on them."

"Possibly. You've got a hunch now?"

"Yes. One I don't like."

She could have followed the line of the particular hunch, and he was ready to talk about it. But instead she moved from the particular to the general.

"What are they?" she mused. "Clairvoyance? Telepathy?"

"I doubt it. Just integration of too many factors for the steps to be remembered. An I.Q. 200 conclusion reached by an I.Q. 140 brain."

She shook her head. "I won't buy that. Low-power, unfocused telepathy seems more reasonable. Let me think about it."

They fell into silence again, Alison lazily arranging all the data her mind contained on hunches, sifting it, reaching conclusions and building up theories.

Raigmore, on the other hand, went back to the particular from the general.

They were at the Hever house, and Gloria was around somewhere and knew where they were. If any information came in she would be with them in a few seconds. Someone would be listening to the radio. But possibly his hunch was about something so apparently trivial, though eventually significant, that no one would bother to tell Gloria or that she wouldn't bother to tell them.

Margo came in quietly. She had changed; she greeted them a little awkwardly, dropped beside Alison and started talking to her. Her behavior wasn't very much different from that of a million other girls in love with another girl's man. She had to be near him; yet when she was near him she wished she hadn't come.

Raigmore looked from Alison to Margo and back again, trying to drive his hunch from his consciousness. Alison could wear anything as if she was doing it a favor. Her plain white swim suit looked no more right or wrong on her than day dress or evening dress. It showed more of her perfect body, but other dress emphasized other points. Surveying Margo in a play suit, Raigmore decided she was best in evening dress. Only dressed as she had been when he first met her did she have anything comparable to the youthful magnificence of Alison.

He heard how adroitly Alison had turned the conversation to Fred, and noted with amusement and admiration how she was drawing Margo into saying anything good that was said about him. Alison said all the things that were on the debit side—how he wouldn't stick to anything, that he wasn't serious enough, that he was lazy. And Margo had to say that he never left anything until it was clear that the people he left doing it were going to finish it successfully; that he was serious enough about the things that mattered, that he never refused to take anything on when it was clear he ought to do it.

Soon Alison, with the ease and concealed art of the White Star, was even making a date with Margo on behalf of Salter. Raigmore was quite interested in the technique Alison was using with a woman who must be no stranger to that technique herself. Alison was handling Margo tactfully, sympathetically, as Margo must have handled scores of Browns and Purples.

But at the back of his mind was the realization that the date wouldn't be kept.

When Gloria came in the two girls merely looked up at her lazily, relaxing in the soporific heat of the July sun. But Raigmore knew even without observing her agitation that this was what he'd been waiting for.

"Robertson is dead," said Gloria bluntly. "Murdered. It was like your father, Alison. They have the man, and he seems to know as little as Brolley did."

Margo screamed.

In another world, or in the same world at another time, the news wouldn't have meant much. Robertson was the President of the United States, but he was only a man. If murder was a comparative commonplace, the murder of anyone, even a President, would just be an incident, no more.

But murder wasn't a commonplace. The death of Banks, discovered, would have shaken a nation. Hever, then Robertson, meant *purpose*. It meant organization. It meant so much more than the mere death of two men.

Raigmore remembered the words spoken in a cabin on a luxury ship. *They will come to give, not to take.* Come to give what?

Murder?

chapter two

RAIGMORE DIDN'T NOTICE GLORIA GO. HE HAD ALLOWED himself to sink so deep in thought that it was a shock when Alison spoke.

"You knew," she said quietly. Margo looked up, startled.

"I knew, but I could do nothing. It might have been that, it might have been anything. As a matter of fact, if I expected anything, it was something quite different."

"What did you expect?"

He saw no reason why he shouldn't tell her. She wasn't looking at Margo, she was looking at him. "Invasion from space," he said.

It was an old story, this fear of invasion. But the fact that it was an old story, a story of which many people were tired, didn't make any difference to its seriousness, should it ever actually happen. People talked glibly about it without ever sitting down seriously to examine it.

He didn't have to tell this to Alison or to Margo. They didn't laugh when he mentioned invasion from space. It was something no one with a culture which was a going concern wanted. Intergalactic trade sounded very fine, but who wanted insecurity and fear and competition and possibly fighting when Earth and Venus and Mars were going along very nicely as they were? Only a comparable civilization would imply benefits in a meeting of peoples. Earth didn't want to subject or to be subjected.

No, the Meeting of Worlds sounded very fine, but nobody wanted it. Earlier or later, perhaps, but not when a civilization had climbed independently as Earth's had done.

Margo and he caught each other's glance for a moment. Margo was only puzzled. She didn't know whether this was a red herring or not. It didn't strike any chord in her. She was just waiting to see what happened.

142

Raigmore knew perfectly well that he was arguing on both sides—on Earth's in his thoughts, and on the invaders' in his actions. Of course, as always, he couldn't know. He might have been placed where he was, to do what he had done, with Earth's interests as his goal. But he couldn't quite believe it.

"It's not that yet, anyway," said Alison, dismissing it. "But it may be almost as big. For someone to kill my father might have been a rare accident. We thought it was. But this shows there must be some plan. It may be America that's being attacked, or the Whites, or law and order, or the whole world."

Raigmore didn't argue. Something in Alison's face puzzled him. "What's wrong?" he asked.

"Don't you see?"

"See what?"

"How this affects you. Two Whites have died. Wars have been started for less, and this may be only the beginning. The White Stars are needed now. You'll be the next President."

He still couldn't see it for a moment. It was difficult to remember how the Tests were trusted. He had an equivocal past, and he was a White Star of only two months. But he was a White Star, and that was all that mattered. The rest had been washed off the slate. What he had been, how little was known of him, how recently he had graduated, were nothing beside that other fact. *He was a White Star!*

Then he saw. Most of the White Stars would be old. Alison was a woman, and there would be irrational prejudice, even now, against appointing a woman in time of danger to face it and handle it, when men hitherto had failed.

He saw the whole plan that had placed him in the present position—saw it in one blinding flash. He had known its general lines for a long time, but he had never seen himself as the supreme leader on Earth. He had thought vaguely that he was meant to climb to the top as a spy—learning, so that he could eventually reveal. He had never seen himself as playing the major part on both sides in the coming struggle.

He wasn't a spy, really. He was a saboteur, on a vast scale. Hever and Robertson had died simply so that he would have the opportunity. Their deaths had been unconnected with him, quite unknown to him until the men were dead. But the two murders had been the work of the party or race which had placed him on Earth.

He drew a deep, shuddering breath, and Alison looked at him sharply. Perhaps she was wondering if it were possible that he was afraid.

He was afraid, though of nothing she could imagine. He was Something Else—the knowledge of that had been left in him. But he was also a man. A man whose world might be about to be invaded by a race who had planned the invasion to the last detail, including putting one of their own people in the position of supreme authority on Earth. A race who could casually produce a White Star to compete with and deceive the best minds that Earth could produce.

It was as if he were working to his own downfall. He thought of himself, suddenly, as an ironworker forging the knife that was to be plunged in his own breast. But a worker who could do nothing else. A worker whose whole life was in the job he was doing.

He didn't notice what happened to Margo. Except for that one scream when Gloria told them what had happened, Margo had stayed out of it. Whatever game Raigmore was playing, it was too deep for her. She must have left them, dressed and gone home.

Raigmore wasn't quite sure himself what game he was playing. But he knew this. He was doing nothing irrevocable against Earth, and all he could to help it, until he knew more. He should have been *Tertium Quid*, sitting on the fence; instead he was out in the open, leading one party and knowing he belonged to the other.

An hour after they heard of Robertson's murder, he and Alison were called to Washington.

chapter three

THE NEXT TWELVE HOURS SHOULD HAVE BEEN IMPRESSIVE.

First there was the hall, the senate house, in which sixty men and women sat, every last one of them wearing a white badge. There were sonorous words—"for the greatest good of mankind," "under the shadow of the greatest crisis of this century," "to protect the right and the just"—and they meant nothing yet, for the senators didn't know what they were talking about. It was even possible, though not likely, that the affair would end here.

Morton, the White Cross Secretary, was saying: ". . . and in this crisis one man must have all power. This *is* a crisis, Senators. Two men like Hever and Robertson aren't assassinated by chance. Something is rocking the foundations of government, and someone must be able to say 'Do this' and know it will be done. I have already explained that in a matter of hours we shall be welcoming representatives of all nations and a world security council will be formed. The President, of course, is Eldin Raigmore, deputy president Alison Hever, their advisers every White Star now living."

Raigmore looked up as a tall man rose, interrupting the Secretary's summary. The indicator before him read Robert Maier and, like Morton, he wore the White Cross. He was an old man, probably over a hundred, but he had vigor and presence. Raigmore recognized personality as the council hushed under the force of Maier's will.

"This world," said Maier loudly, scathingly, "deserves all that is undoubtedly coming to it. Two men die. We are stampeded into appointing a dictator. And who is the dictator? A man who was a Black only a few months ago. A man who called himself Joe Banks."

He looked round the room, compelling silence and attention by very will. "I have nothing against undocumented Blacks," he went on ironically, "they can be remarkable men. We know that because one of them has become a White Star—by definition, above us all."

Suddenly he shouted. "Do you not see, wise men, that Hever and Robertson died for a purpose? They died so that sooner or later *their* man—the agent of the murderers—

would attain power." He paused, went on more quietly: "I don't say we have reached him yet. Raigmore may die too, and then we shall know he was innocent. But at last we shall appoint a leader—President, dictator, controller, supervisor, what you will—who will not die. Nor will he make mistakes. The enemy we are fighting has made none, and is not likely to start now."

His voice rose again. "We will not lose this battle, wise men. I tell you the grim truth that you will not face—we have lost it now!"

As Maier sat down, Raigmore looked round cautiously and saw the incredible truth—that Maier's outburst had made no effect at all. The Secretary was resuming where he left off, and after a slightly embarrassed pause the senators were drawing their attention back to Morton's words.

Suddenly Raigmore understood. A hundred years or more ago, when Maier was born, the Tests had been a great boon, a mighty mark of progress, but not yet a part of every man's beliefs. Maier was the only man who could speak as he did because he was perhaps the only White left who could think as he did about the Tests.

The answer of the others to Maier's tirade, if they had thought it needed an answer, would have been on the lines: "The old man seems to forget that we are not putting our trust in ordinary men, but in White Stars. True, even they may fail. But if they do, so should we."

And their attitude, Raigmore realized, was the right one—now. For the tiny alteration he had made in the Tests—his thesis had been examined, commended and immediately acted on—meant that now they were all these Whites believed. Their attitude, though they could not know it, was wrong only in that Raigmore, the man into whose hands they were putting the future of the world, had been selected on an imperfect system.

". . . White Stars," said Morton. "Why the two youngest were chosen is obvious. In the first place, what has happened, as we all realize, is only the prelude to something bigger. The duration may be a week or a hundred years. Naturally we put our trust in a man who may live through it, not an old man who must die in twenty years. Moreover, action, decision, even impetuosity are required—though only the impetuosity of a White Star. So we would have chosen Eldin Raigmore in any case.

"But there was a second factor. When we asked the opinion of the other White Stars, they were unanimous. Remember, even we haven't quite the selflessness of the highest and greatest minds of our time. They knew the maturity of the human mind, and they knew its youth. Their verdict—put our trust in the youngest male White Star, aided by the youngest female White Star, and replace them if necessary through the entire ranks of the group in reverse order of seniority."

One couldn't say this time, Raigmore thought, that the gravity of the situation hadn't been realized. Often in the past the signs of coming disaster had been plainer and far more numerous, and nothing had been done. But this time, on no more than two incidents, strong action was being taken.

And the decision was right. Raigmore knew it was right.

The ceremony went on, and presently Raigmore saw Maier rise in disgust and leave the chamber. Raigmore looked across at Alison, and she smiled back. He saw someone who had noticed the exchange frown reprovingly. Raigmore wondered if he really thought grim expressions were going to help. Alison was hardly even listening to the proceedings. Nothing was said, no decision was reached which had not already been agreed. She and Raigmore were there to be installed, and anything more than a ten-word statement of the fact was so much effort wasted.

She was, of course, perfectly right.

The ceremony, however, dragged itself along like a wounded animal. It finished at last in the late afternoon. In the evening there was more ceremony—introductions, suggestions, meetings, presentations. Raigmore's attitude by now was the twin of Alison's. These things had to happen. They were expected, they were even necessary. He and Alison wouldn't be properly installed, the people would never believe they were really their new leaders, if all this ceremony was cut out.

Meeting so many White Circles and Crosses, Raigmore had a striking demonstration of a Test truism—no one was so far below one as the people just one step below. Whites were seldom conscious of being *above* other people. They were merely aware, generally, of difference. But the White Crosses, even Morton, seemed to bustle about so, and be upset by little things, and have such a love of ceremony, that Raigmore couldn't help regarding them as rather petty creatures, like the lizard juror in *Alice in Wonderland*. They all seemed to be looking for lost pencils, or writing on their slates with one finger. He knew this was a fallacy. However, it was certainly the way it looked.

It was only after all this that Raigmore was able to get anything done. It was late, but he had sent for Salter, Gloria and Margo.

In a tiny room almost lost among all the huge council chambers and offices, he told them why. "We five know each other pretty well," he said. "Whatever happens, I want us to stay together and work together. I think we'll do better work than any other existing unit."

"Do you think anything is going to happen?" Gloria asked.

"I do. And soon. Fred, I want you to stick with me pretty well all the time. And Margo, you stay with Alison. Hever and Robertson were each killed by one man who knew what to do to get them alone. I don't think anything more will be learned from this Jim Kempson than from Brolley. Like Brolley, the man who killed Robertson is quite insignificant, just a robot trained to kill.

"I think Alison and I will be safe enough if no insignificant little creature like Brolley or Kempson gets near us, alone."

There was even more to it than that. If Salter was always with him, and Margo with Alison, that meant human with spy, canceling each other.

"That's sound," said Salter. "I'll stick to you like a shadow, Raigmore. Don't worry—I'll look after you."

"I mean that," Raigmore insisted, looking at Margo. "Kempson knew exactly where and when to find Robertson alone. If Alison looks into a cupboard, Margo, you look

into it first. I don't think it will be dangerous for you—
Kempson and Brolley got the men they wanted. If she goes
back for a coat, you go with her. Don't go for it and don't
let her go for it alone."

Margo nodded.

"And what do I do?" asked Gloria.

"You're head of communications, Gloria."

"Am I? Since when?"

"Since a moment ago. Will you take the job? Good. I
want you because you don't have to be told how to do
things. Arrange your own communications bureau . . ."

He didn't know Gloria as well as he knew the others, for
she spoke very little and always effaced herself when she
was in a group. It wasn't because she was shy. She was
always cool, serene, mildly interested in everything. She
was pretty but it took you weeks to notice it. Raigmore was
fairly certain she would be more efficient than anyone else
in the job he had given her. A Yellow Star, she would be
more efficient, probably, than a White, because she would
work harder at it. The method of the White would be to
arrange things beautifully and then sit back and let his
machine run. Gloria would keep at it.

Gloria set to work at once, but the others slept in three
rooms in the administration building itself. Anyone who
reached Alison and Raigmore would have to pass through
first Salter's room and then Margo's.

It was as Raigmore and Alison were dressing the next
morning that the first reports of attack began to come in
from Mars.

chapter four

IT WAS QUITE A DRAMA, THE STORY TOLD BY THOSE MESSAGES from Mars. When Raigmore saw them they were already complete. The record ran:

0300 HOURS MARS TIME: New London reporting per James Harker, chief radio officer. Fleet detected beyond Jupiter approaching at speed of approximately 90,000 miles per second, therefore obviously extrasolar system. Deceleration rapid and too intense for human body. Preliminary estimate indicates Mars is objective.

0400 HOURS MT: New London, per James Harker. Fleet estimated at one thousand ships. Mars now obvious objective, unless course is changed suddenly. Fleet still decelerating. Expected here within half an hour at present rate of deceleration. First force field building up at million-mile radius from Mars. Second field ready.

0426 HOURS: Entire fleet through field without apparent damage. Field was at full strength, designed to overload all electrical apparatus, detonate all explosives, ignite all highly combustible substances and break down any instable elements. Fleet entering second field.

0428 HOURS: Pardon me if I drop formality, but it's all over. The alien fleet is not only through the so-called impenetrable second shield, it's maneuvering in it. So unless they're friendly—and I'm no incorrigible optimist—it's good-by Mars and good-by Earth, and we might as well have been still in our caves for all the good four or five centuries of scientific progress has done us. Did someone say we still have our weapons of attack, though defense has failed? Brother, all our knowledge of attack is in our defense screens. If they come through them without as much as noticing—and they might as well not have been on for all the difference it made, as far as I could see—we might as well save ourselves the trouble of taking our peashooter shots at them. We . . .

0430 HOURS: Canallon reporting, per Robert Myles, second radio officer. All communication from the hemisphere of Mars facing the alien fleet has ceased—telephone, radio, everything. Power on the universal link-up has gone too, but we're working on our own generators. There has been no seismographic shock. No one here has been affected in any way, and it appears that power has been mopped up or frozen by . . . One ship has appeared over the horizon. No sign of a ray or beam or . . .

0431 HOURS: San Martin reporting, per it doesn't matter who now. No ships in sight yet, and as we have to try something we're working on the theory that the invaders are using some kind of a beam that can be stopped by some sort of shielding. So we have as protection first a Darkness shield, shunting any overload power into the universal power link-up—that probably won't do any harm now— then the glass dome of this station sprayed with everything we can think of—reflecting paint on the outside, and under that weatherproofing, conductor, heat insulation and radioactivity shield. On the inside there are things nobody has had time to tell me about, but if it works we'll tell you and you can take the whole thing as a unit. Shutting down now because we're putting up a radio screen that'll stop even our signals. We'll let it down for a second in half an hour's time to let through our call sign, and even if that lets the invaders get us, you'll know our defenses have worked. But as we won't let down anything but the radio screen there isn't much risk. Signing off.

0431 HOURS: Butler Bay reporting. We're going underground, twenty of us, through the old coal workings. The intervention of a section of the planet seems to be some protection, so we mean to get sixteen miles down. We're taking a small radio—you'll have to step up the power to hear us, but you should get our signals all right if we're still safe. Signing off.

0433 HOURS: Oscar City reporting. No ships in sight here yet. We're taking off in a ship of our own, forty of us, when I get through with this message. By the time the aliens see us, if they ever do, we should have escape velocity and be headed for Earth. So you may learn something from the ship. Signing off.

That was all. One hour and thirty-three minutes after the ships were sighted, the last messages from Mars were coming in. One hour and thirty-four minutes, and Mars was dead, as far as Earth was concerned. There was no sign of the Oscar City ship.

Raigmore immediately convened a meeting of the new world security council. He sent for Salter, because he knew Mars, and told him to bring Margo with him; Mallin, the next White Star in line should anything happen to him or Alison; the top echelon of science and law and order—not the military, for there was no military, but the police. They were together in less than two hours and Raigmore took his seat with Alison on his right. In private life she might be his wife, but here she was his second in command—and there might be no private life ever again.

"First, Mallin," he said, and looked at the man. He was

about forty, the probable leader in this emergency if Raigmore had not been there to complicate matters. He would have been a good leader, Raigmore thought, surveying him. Perhaps Raigmore's sole purpose had been to prevent Mallin leading the defense against the invaders.

"I can't give you orders, Mallin," he said. "You know the circumstances, and I needn't reiterate them. I can only suggest to you, of all people, what I think would be a good idea and see if you agree."

Mallin nodded. "But I think I'd accept your orders, Raigmore," he remarked. "I wasn't actually among the group that selected you, but I was a party to the decision. Go ahead."

"If we're going to be a pushover for the invaders," said Raigmore, "we must at least try to ensure the survival of the race. I think that's agreed. I want you to attend to that, Mallin. I want you to select a group, twenty, a hundred or a thousand, balanced or unbalanced according to your own fancy, and take them to some place of safety. While you still can. It may, of course, be already too late. And we may also find the invaders far less of a problem than we imagine at the moment. But I think this is one thing that has to be done."

Mallin nodded. "I agree. I'll go at once. Where do you suggest we go?"

"I'm going to be most careful not to suggest anywhere. And I don't want you to tell me a thing—not even who goes with you. You can have anyone you like, bar Alison and myself. And you can take them where you like. But tell no one who remains where you are going, inside this system or outside it. What the invaders may learn from us we don't know. We don't even know what they want. They may be perfectly satisfied with Mars. But in case they would follow you, we must know nothing. You agree?"

"Naturally," said Mallin. He rose. "I won't waste any time. We won't communicate with you in any way until we are sure it's safe. Good-by, Raigmore."

He rose and left the chamber. And with his going Raigmore knew he had noticeably weakened Earth. Either way, however, it was necessary.

"Next," he said. "Salter, you know Mars. Perhaps there is something in those last messages that suggests something to you that the rest of us don't see."

Salter rose. There was no laziness about him now. "There's a lot in those messages," he said, "but because time is short I won't say much about how they show that even in their last moments the men on Mars tried everything that they thought might give us a line. I don't think in an emergency a group of people ever showed up better. But you can all see that. What I want to say is something you should all have been able to see too, but apparently nobody has."

Raigmore nodded. "I think I know what you mean," he said. "I'm glad someone agrees with me. If it's the same thing."

It was a lie. He had intended to keep it to himself for a while, given the opportunity. Since he wasn't given the opportunity, he had to play along with Salter and confirm his conclusions.

Salter stared hard at him. "Yes, you would see it, Raig-

more," he admitted. "How about you, Alison? Or any of
the rest of you?"

"If this is some sort of test," said Alison, "I've failed it.
Unless what you have to say is something I've simply been
taking for granted."

"No," said Salter. "It's this. The messages seem to show
that the alien ships' weapons, whatever they are, work in
a direct line through air but not through the body of Mars.
The message from Butler Bay says as much. After there
was complete silence from nearly half of the planet, we were
still receiving messages from the other half, until a ship or
ships got round to dealing with it. It's unlikely that the
invaders'—let's call it a beam till we know better—it's unlikely that their beam was deliberately aimed at only that
part of Mars which they could see and not intended to
paralyze the other side of the planet. If they could have
switched off the whole planet in one instant, they'd have
done it. Instead, they picked it off a little at a time."

He paused. Alison looked at Raigmore and saw that
Salter's line of argument was clear to him, looked at the
others in the room and saw they were as puzzled as she was.

"Go on," she said.

"You know the preparations that were made at San
Martin and Butler Bay," Salter continued. "You may say
the Butler Bay party never had time to get underground.
I don't believe it. The message from Oscar City indicates
they must have had at least three minutes, probably more.
That's time enough to get well down the sixteen-mile shaft
at the full power of the elevators. They could work them
off their own generators like the radio. And give them

credit for the sense to close the shaft behind them. But if you want to write off the Butler Bay group, pin everything on what happened at San Martin. We haven't heard anything from them—not even the call sign they promised. Why, in heaven's name? Their preparations must have protected them twice as well as any mere intervention of a slice of rock and earth. That insulation——"

"I see," said Alison. She couldn't be said to be excited, but she was more excited than Raigmore had ever seen her. "But the beam could be limited purely by distance——"

"You wouldn't say that if you knew Mars. Canallon went off the air just after 0430. San Martin signed off, still safe, at 0433. And San Martin is between Canallon and New London. The invaders' beam should have cut San Martin off before Canallon, or at least at the same time. Why the lag? Because the beam was lapping San Martin and doing no damage. Or even because there was no beam."

The chamber buzzed, people who thought they understood explaining to people who were still puzzled.

"In short," Raigmore said, taking up Salter's story, "it's not as we imagined at first, that the invaders simply turned on their beam and anything in its path was finished. What Salter has said *may* only mean that the invaders have a beam which can be stopped only by distance or the intervention of sufficient solid matter or its equivalent, in the case of San Martin. Then, when they know that it has failed, they use a second beam which wipes up what they have missed. But I don't think Salter believes that, and neither do I."

"Think!" exclaimed Salter. "Count out distance. The

beam works—we don't yet know what it does—over a vast area, stopped only by a shield of matter. But San Martin and Butler Bay weren't saved by that shield. So we are supposed to think that there's no defense against the invaders. No shield that they can't batter down or penetrate. But that's wrong. What's the truth?"

"In a word, sabotage," said Alison. She said it quite coolly, accepting the fantastic implications because the line of reasoning demanded them. But there were no other White Stars in the room except Raigmore, now that Mallin had gone. The others couldn't accept the answer as she did.

Raigmore called for order. "Salter's perfectly right," he said. "Remember, we've proved nothing yet—this is only a theory. But remember what Harker said? The defense screens might as well not have been on for all the difference it made.

"I don't believe they were on at all."

He had gone a step farther than Salter, he saw. Perhaps later he would regret having said this. But it seemed to him inevitable. On the evidence before him, he had to draw that conclusion. Alison would, if he didn't.

He decided, however, not to go further still—yet. After all, it might transpire that this was all for Earth's benefit. He doubted it more and more, but . . .

He looked at Margo. She was nodding. He interpreted that to mean she agreed with his casting in his lot with Earth. But that relieved him of no responsibility.

The council was still in uproar at what he had said, and he was doing nothing about it. Now of all times he wished passionately that he knew more. Here and now, he thought, he could tip the scale one way or the other by what he did or didn't do.

And he didn't know which way to tip it.

chapter five

THE MEETING BROKE UP, VERY NEARLY IN DISORDER. RAIG-more let it break up. Curiously enough, more than half the members still seemed suspicious of Salter's conclusion and Raigmore's acceptance of it. They felt they were being pushed into something. They distrusted what they couldn't understand.

But Raigmore knew the White Stars would be with him when the warning went forth. They would agree that Salter's theory was the best one to work on. So would the council, eventually. They merely had to be left alone, given time to get used to the idea. Lower down in the scale of intelligence, people would believe, as they always had, what they were told.

Raigmore wanted time too. He didn't want to do anything irrevocable, either way. So he didn't point out yet, as he could have done, that to be sure that Martian attack would go the way they wanted it to go the invaders must have had at least a thousand saboteurs there. Nor that Earth, on the same basis, must have tens of thousands of them. . . .

Left with Alison, Salter, Gloria, Margo and Morton, he

was as noncommittal as he could possibly be with such a group. He was certain he was with them; but he was determined not to back one side completely before hearing the other's case.

"We may have only a few hours' grace," he said, "and we're faced with perhaps the greatest case of subtlety in history. We not only have to work out what to think, but what we're probably meant to think. And point one is whether we're supposed to have seen what you worked out, Fred, or not."

"Look how nearly we didn't," objected Alison.

"On the other hand," said Gloria, "if they made it clearer we might have refused to consider it."

Morton cleared his throat and spoke. "I'm ready to take this theory about spies as a working hypothesis," he said. "But I know why the others weren't. The New London operator pointed out that the rate of deceleration of the ships indicated pretty clearly that the creatures inside couldn't be human. Now we're saying that some of them are among us and we've never known it."

They went on talking round the point, Raigmore doing his best, reluctantly, to keep them at it. Morton wanted to expand the defense forces, the fleet, everything. Raigmore told him to do that only on the basis of keeping the whole force balanced.

"Don't double it for a ten-per-cent increase in efficiency," he said. "That's all right when your force can acquire battle experience fairly easily and cheaply. I don't think that's going to be possible this time."

"If the invaders appear over Washington in the next few

minutes," said Morton, harassed, "what are we going to *do?*"

"Nothing," said Raigmore, "in the next five minutes. Earth's defense, such as it is, is best left alone for the moment. We can multiply it in power, but we can't alter it in kind. If the invaders attack at once, we have to let the present defense force do what they can."

He managed more or less to maintain the *status quo*. Morton was left to expand all forces cautiously; Raigmore said that was all that could be done for the moment. It wasn't, of course. He could have pointed out that if the saboteurs existed, and if they had insinuated themselves into Earth's defenses, the thing to do was to change the defense personnel everywhere as far as possible—merely to change it, since any change must be for the better.

He wanted to work wholeheartedly for Earth. But he felt that in his ignorance he couldn't—and that soon, very soon, he must have more information to work on. If he was there with a purpose, he calculated that it was just about time he was told what that purpose was. Already he had had chances which he hadn't taken.

"Now I think we should break up and get some sleep," he said. Waiting for the exact text of the Mars reports, getting the council together, holding the meeting and the discussion after it had somehow run away with the whole day. And though they didn't feel that much had been done, they were tired.

"Sleep!" muttered Morton.

Raigmore surveyed him with a grim smile. "Do you think you'll be better able to deal with an attack tomorrow or the next day if you don't?"

Salter took Raigmore a little ahead of Alison and Margo as they made their way to their bedrooms.

"Shouldn't you and Alison stay well apart for the time being, Raigmore?" he asked quietly, not at all like the lazy, cheerful Salter Raigmore knew. "If you stay together, a well-placed bomb or a couple of quick shots will mean we're looking for another leader. Hadn't you better send Margo and Alison somewhere else, to some other city—Millo, perhaps?"

Raigmore shook his head. "I see your point, Fred," he admitted, "but I want Alison around. If something does happen soon, we want a compact little force, the five of us, to be ready to act together. Besides . . ."

He hesitated, working out how to say what he meant to say so that it would make sense to Salter. "There's another thing, Fred," he said at last. "We agreed that the whole Mars affair was principally a demonstration, didn't we? That it was arranged so that we would think the invaders were invincible?"

"Well, that's one possibility," Salter said. "There are others."

"Right. Suppose it was a demonstration. What's the point of a demonstration like that?"

"Psychological. To show us there's no use trying."

"With what purpose?"

Salter stopped. "You've got something up your sleeve. Hadn't we better get the girls in this?"

Raigmore took his arm and led him on. "I don't want the girls in this if I can help it. What purpose would there be in showing us there's no use trying?"

Salter was puzzled. "To make us surrender easily, I expect," he said.

"Exactly. Then don't you think that someone may possibly give us the chance?"

"Now, you mean? Before an attack on Earth?"

"Yes."

Salter considered that. He nodded. "It won't work, of course," he said. "We obviously aren't going to surrender. But the invaders, whoever they are, might try it."

Raigmore didn't know whether he was at last remembering things from before May 23, or just working them out for himself. But he was sure now that the invaders would try to make contact with him, their man, in a matter of hours. He wanted them to do it. He wanted it desperately.

And he had to make it possible for them to do it.

He didn't know how the contact would be achieved. But certainly it would have to be done secretly, for if he was to remain useful to them, as Earth's leader, there must be no suspicion that he was a spy. Someone had to get to him alone and unknown, and that might not be possible if Salter continued to guard him closely.

"I agree with what you said this far," Raigmore went on. "Alison can sleep where we were last night, and I'll go somewhere else in the building. But if anyone comes to see me, I want you to let him through."

"Are you crazy?" Salter demanded. "That's exactly how——"

"That's exactly how I think a surrender ultimatum would be delivered to us. We know the invaders have agents here, and they must know what's going on. If they have anything to say, they'll come to me."

Raigmore had to argue for quite a while before Salter began to see that there might be something in what he said. And Alison, sensing that something was going on, joined them in the middle of the discussion, looking from one to the other.

"What's the argument?" she asked.

Raigmore recognized at once that he wasn't going to be able to arrange things quite as he wanted. Some women might be fobbed off with a casual lie, but not Alison. Reluctantly he told her what he had told Salter.

"I think you're right," said Alison briskly. "Now that that's settled, let's go to bed."

Raigmore frowned. "You mean . . ."

"I mean, let's make it possible for a spy to come and see us if he likes. Fred and Margo can stay out of the way."

Fred protested, but Raigmore was prepared to accept the compromise. He had to be; there was no shifting Alison. He knew she would be safe whatever happened, because she represented part of his power.

Naturally Margo and particularly Fred remained a little puzzled by the situation. That couldn't be helped. It wasn't possible always to kill two birds with one stone, to find some course—like the dispatch of Mallin from Earth—which was satisfactory from all points of view. It was as a game of chess must look to chessmen endowed with intelligence but not full perception. They wouldn't understand why a queen should be risked for no obvious, immediate gain.

They wouldn't see that the queen, as it happened, was safe, because things were arranged so that more would be lost in capturing her than could possibly be gained. Alison sensed something of that.

Perhaps it was because she did that she said later, when she and Raigmore were alone in their bedroom: "There's more in this than you're telling me, Eldin, isn't there?"

She was looking at him steadily. Raigmore admitted it at once. "But there's a good reason for not telling you, Alison," he added.

"You mean I might not do the right thing if I knew?"

"Something like that. Will you trust me?"

She smiled faintly. "That's a silly question. I may think you're wrong, but there's no question of not trusting you."

Raigmore hoped that nothing would ever happen to change that.

chapter six

RAIGMORE ONLY PRETENDED TO SLEEP. WITH EVERY PASSING moment he became surer that this was the time for him to be told the truth.

Alison was asleep. Her shoulder and arm seemed to catch all the light in the room. Not a yard from him was a woman who loved him, trusted him completely. That was more than he did—he could hardly trust himself.

He went over all the old arguments in his mind. He had

nothing to add to them, but he repeated them over and over again as if something would suddenly click and everything that had happened to him would mean something clear and sensible.

He had done nothing so far aimed against the human race. That, he knew, was one of the reasons why the Tests had passed him. That was necessary. He had done nothing against humanity and he intended to do nothing against it. Neither did Margo, he knew. The old question came up again—did that mean that the invaders, after all, were friendly, even philanthropic, as what Carter had said implied? They had taken Mars, true, but no one knew that they had harmed a single human being there.

Perhaps he could have the best of both worlds. Perhaps he could fight for the two races together, somehow. But first he had to know. He had to know *now*.

He must have sensed what was happening, or what was just going to happen. It could not have been mere coincidence that what happened happened precisely then.

It was the agony of death. He was fighting and failing. Struggling, failing, weakening.

It was less weakening than dissolving, falling apart. Raigmore, that artificial creature, was disintegrating into its component parts.

The two Nwyllans were looking through the same window at the same thing, but what they saw was entirely different. Eavl or Yafl saw two strangely complicated animals, tiring to the eye in their complexity, and wearing shaped coverings that were more complex still. Ufd or Oovt saw Alison Raigmore, née Hever, and what had lately been himself.

The quiescence of the two creatures, too, meant nothing to Eavl. The animals he was watching might be engaged in their most violent activity. After all, the smaller one was quite visibly moving. The twin protuberances a little below what Ufd said was a head were rising and falling rhythmically and every now and then the whole organism would shudder.

But Ufd knew that Alison was just coming out of the induced trance which had enabled the Nwyllans to take her with the body of Raigmore to their ship, now five million miles above Earth. Saboteurs—Ufd now knew them by their Nwyllan names—had worked to a timetable prepared years in advance to let Eavl's ship through Earth's defenses twice without any Terran knowing it was there. That was Nwyllan planning.

The two Earth creatures lay on couches hurriedly constructed at Ufd's order. Alison wore a green nightdress and Raigmore vivid pajamas. But they would not be cold, even when they awoke, for the temperature in the room was boiling hot to a Nwyllan, heavily pressurized, and had a very low gravity.

As they watched coldly, Alison opened her eyes and sat up, shaking her head. Still half asleep, she seemed surprised that there was no covering over her. She tried several times to push aside something that wasn't there.

Then she was awake, and Ufd glanced curiously at his colleague. It seemed incredible that even a Nwyllan could be indifferent to Alison's beauty.

But that was, of course, twisted thinking. Ufd was half a man, half a Nwyllan. His tough, incredibly simple body, one trunk and many legs, like an inverted tree, would be startling to Alison, if not frightening, but to him she was still the same as ever. He was not Ufd, but Ufd-Raigmore, and since the Raigmore part was so much more recent, he was really more Raigmore than Ufd. Alison was still, he thought with humor, his wife. Humor experienced in a Nwyllan body was a new thing to him. It was not in the Nwyllan catalogue of experience—*but it was possible.* Ufd saw some of the significance.

The Nwyllans stood where they were, watching. The glass was one-way. The Earth creatures would not know they were observed.

Alison saw Raigmore and leapt with a cry to his side. Ufd knew she had cried out, because he was watching her. The glass cut off sound, but even if it had not, Ufd would have heard nothing. No Nwyllan except himself had ever heard a sound, nor could conceive it. No Nwyllan had ever consciously eaten, or spoken, or smelled anything, or tasted. They ate, certainly, through their pores—but that was an unconscious process, and the Nwyllans had had to travel far above their primitive state millions of years ago before they learned that they lived by absorbing bacteria. Just as a man could breathe without having learned of the existence of air, the Nwyllans had renewed their energy without knowing that their energy had to be renewed.

Alison soon found that Raigmore's trance was of a different order from her own. She got him awake after a fashion, but at first all he could do was gasp and writhe. Ufd saw the misery on her face and realized with surprise and intense interest that he, in his Nwyllan body, could still feel sympathy and pity and love, a thing no other Nwyllan had ever done.

Presently the mindless thing in the room with Alison felt stirrings of a sex impulse and began to claw at the girl. She evaded him for a while, then, her face still racked with horror and sadness, she tied him with strips she tore from his pajama jacket.

Ufd spoke to Eavl mentally. "My knowledge is returning rapidly, but reminding me of things helps. What are we going to do with these people?"

"I can guess at your state of mind," replied Eavl, "when you use for them a concept 'people' which has hitherto been applied only to Nwyllans. I admit you are right. They are intelligent—they are undoubtedly 'people.' But it would never have occurred to me to refer to them as such. What are we going to do with them? On Mars we found no White Stars, as you call them, and we must find out from the smaller creature what being a White Star implies. You were a White Star too, but that means nothing. You would be one of our White Stars, if we used a grading system. You say none of our people were White Stars among these creatures?"

"I knew one who was a Brown—at the bottom in the human scale. There are nearly fifty thousand, you say. None of them is a White Star, and few of them are Whites, if any."

"Then the humans, as we thought, are more than worthy

of inclusion in our worlds. They are our equals, in fact, save for their emotion."

The Nwyllans thought not in words, for words could not evolve among a race who had never heard sound, but in concepts. There had to be some standardization of concepts for understanding, and Ufd saw that emotion, a new concept, was standardized meantime as something like "acting irrationally for possibly valid reasons at present beyond our comprehension." There was a contradiction in the idea of acting irrationally for reasons, but that arose through the standardization of the concepts "irrational" and "reasons," and was no contradiction to a Nwyllan. It would be a hard job interpreting Nwyllans to humans, and vice versa.

"Will you help me to run the tests?" asked Eavl.

Ufd needed time to think. "No, but I'll join you later," he said, and turned away.

He went to his room in the huge Nwyllan vessel and relaxed comfortably. This he did by letting his trunk down among his legs, which loosened themselves too, merely having to hold his trunk upright.

From the moment when he had found himself in his own body, he had begun to remember. He still knew everything that had happened to Raigmore; now he knew, as well, what had gone before that. All knowledge of Nwylla had been blocked in Raigmore's mind so that, whatever happened, he could reveal nothing of it to any human being.

He knew now that the Nwyllans had been preparing for many Earth years for their conquest of this particular civilization. They had captured quite a few explorers in the outer regions of the solar system. Then they had begun to make Raigmore and fifty thousand others. Raigmore had learned all that was general in the minds of those explorers, all that they knew except what concerned mere individuals. That was his encyclopedic knowledge, the knowledge that had enabled him from the first to pass as a human being. He *was* a human being.

Any race must have two drives—one toward survival and one toward something else. Self- or race-preservation isn't enough. There must be something else to reinforce it, to help to develop the mind. With some races it might be art, with others sex, with still others merely a universal curiosity. With races like the humans it might be a lot of things.

But among the Nwyllans it was simple. Their secondary drive was toward Empire. The galaxy was gradually becoming filled with races which owed allegiance to Nwylla. What good did it do Nwylla? No more than art or sex or satisfied curiosity did other races. It just had to be done. It was part of existence.

What had enabled the Nwyllans to achieve the successes they had achieved was principally their spy and sabotage system. Fifty thousand Nwyllans had been assigned to the job of bringing Earth into the Empire. Most of the fifty thousand were on Earth now, some knowing no more than Raigmore had, but each ready to play his part when that part became clear. Fifty thousand less the thousand who had been on Mars. They had already done their job and, like Raigmore, were back in their own Nwyllan bodies.

The Nwyllans' espionage system always worked because it had been developed not for one campaign but for every possible campaign. The spies could never be discovered, for they were genuine members of the race which was to be subjected. Here, their children, if they had any, would be human children; they had human bodies, human minds, and only the vaguest knowledge that they had another purpose to fulfill. For each of them, however, the time would come, as it had with Raigmore, when they were called back to their own bodies.

Ufd went all over the system and could see only one flaw in it. Soon he—as Raigmore—and Alison would be returned to Earth. The Nwyllans would make some sort of attack. The attack in itself was of very little importance—the real battle was in the ranks of the defenders, with Nwyllan agents making certain that the battle was lost.

The flaw, the thing that was different this time, was that one of the Nwyllans' own men had turned against them. Ufd wondered why it had never happened before. He soon saw why. Previous races conquered by the Nwyllans had had loyalty to each other, but not this fantastic love of freedom which men had; not the warm emotions of humans. The result, this time, was that the very Nwyllan agents had fallen victim to the disease. Raigmore wanted to be human, to be free, and he wanted Earth to be free. He wanted it so strongly that even Ufd felt the same things.

There had never been any conflict. From the moment when he knew the truth he had wanted victory and freedom for Earth.

chapter seven

THE QUESTION WAS, COULD IT BE DONE? WAS IT POSSIBLE?

Ufd put aside all thought of being a traitor to his own race. Sometimes it wasn't a bad thing to be a traitor to your race—if it was wrong.

Regarding the Nwyllans as wrong, Ufd knew that he was seeing them through the eyes of a man. So perhaps he wasn't a traitor, after all. Even as Ufd, back in the body of a Nwyllan, he thought of the humans as his race.

He could see the Nwyllan point of view too, of course. He knew now why Carter had said, "They will come to benefit Earth. They will come to give, not to take." That was what the Nwyllans thought they were doing. In their view, any race was better off as a member of the Nwyllan Empire than it could ever be otherwise. On Nwyllan premises, that was true. The Nwyllan worlds were safe, well ordered, their resources fully developed. . . .

The fact that these races resisted Nwylla, fighting against her instead of joining her Empire freely, meant no more than a wounded animal's struggle against a man who was trying to help it—and would be paid no more attention.

From many points of view the Nwyllan Empire was a beautiful thing. It meant the end of war, progress, collaboration instead of undirected effort. Human beings, however, were so made that they would always prefer freedom to that kind of security. They insisted on their right to make their own heaven or their own hell.

But that was a matter which could be considered much later, after all this was over. In a struggle like this Ufd had to back one side or the other, and he was backing Earth.

Little things were sliding into place, like why he had attempted to break into Banks's mind. That was a fragment of Nwyllan memory. The Nwyllans were telepaths, and Raigmore, vaguely, must have remembered fighting with his mind. In danger, under stress, he had tried to beat down Banks's brain with his own.

Emotion—naturally he had planned emotionlessly at first. It was only later, gradually, that he had begun to *feel*. His body wasn't a copy of a human body; in every respect it was a human body. In so far as the emotions were physical, Raigmore and Margo experienced them like everyone else. Why Peach and Carter didn't was not clear. But quite possibly it was because greater capacity meant greater adaptability; Raigmore and Margo had adapted to the new conditions, while Peach and Carter had been incapable of it.

The Nwyllans had learned the art of duplication of any life form from one of the first and greatest races they had conquered. This time they had duplicated too well. Raigmore had become a man.

Ufd went back to Eavl. Terrans would be astonished to find that these great ships were each controlled by one being. There was nothing really strange about it when that one Nwyllan could control everything by thought. If the master thought-control system went wrong—then the trouble would start. But if it failed in any one ship, and that was rare, another ship came alongside, and soon everything was in order again.

Eavl acknowledged his return with a formal thought of greeting. He had shut off the one-way block at the inspection window, Ufd saw, so that Alison could see through it too. Beside her on the couch was a pattern test which she was ignoring, as Ufd had known she would. She was staring calmly at Eavl, and now at Ufd, as he joined him.

Ufd was struck by the irony of making a White Star do a test like that. The Earth Tests were recent in his mind, and here was the start of the Nwyllan version, designed to learn the capacities of an individual, whatever the race. The pattern test was simply a board containing interchangeable colored squares almost making up a pattern but not quite. It would be the work of a moment for Alison to correct the errors. It would, in fact, be easier for her than for a Nwyllan.

Of all the senses, Terran and Nwyllan, only one was common—sight. It was not only common, it was almost identical, within the same range. But while to a Nwyllan it would be a simple mental exercise to see a pattern and what was wrong with it, it was hardly a mental exercise at all to a human. Humans were trained from the cradle to the grave in some form or other of artistic appreciation, whether they knew it or not. It would require hardly any mental effort on Alison's part to do what was asked of her.

But she did nothing, waiting.

Eavl gave a mental command and the couch with Raigmore's half-conscious body on it swung out of the way and into a compartment by itself. Another order, and the temperature in the pressurized room sank. Emotionlessly, Eavl was supplying Alison with a motive for doing the test. The temperature, Ufd guessed, dropped a degree a second or slightly over. Alison shivered, but she would not be really cold until a lot of surface temperature had left her. That wouldn't be long. Her nylon nightdress was no insulation whatever against cold. Involuntarily she pulled it about her, but Ufd could see her skin shivering under the material. Still she looked steadily at Eavl.

"It can't take much more of that," Ufd warned.

Eavl gave another order and the temperature visibly mounted again. Ice which had begun to form at the edges of the window rapidly melted, and for a moment the view was obscured by water vapor. Alison flushed crimson as the blood rushed to her skin. Presently she was bathed in sweat and breathing with difficulty. Her nightdress hung damp and limp about her.

Once more Ufd gave a warning, and Eavl started the cycle again. He didn't seem to know, but Ufd did, that these tactics would not be enough. Most White Stars had remarkable control over their bodies. Alison could take this for days.

But it was necessary for him and Alison to get back to Earth. And before Eavl would allow that—for after all, Eavl was under orders—Alison had to run through the Nwyllan equivalent of the Tests—naturally much simpler than the Terran variety, for there was so much less the Nwyllans had to test.

"Have you tried mental contact?" Ufd asked

"Yes, without success. It is no telepath, but it has strength of mind enough to keep me out."

Keep *you* out, Ufd thought. But you've never been a Terran.

With infinite caution he reached out to Alison's mind unknown to the Nwyllan. He had the telepathic abilities of Ufd-Raigmore, and he needed them to deceive a member of a telepathic race.

"Don't reveal anything," he told her. "Just keep on staring at Eavl. Don't try to answer."

Being puzzled didn't make Alison precipitate. Not by the flicker of an eyelid did she reveal that she had been told anything. But she had—the contact was two-way. Ufd felt in his own mind for the first time her characteristic courage and curiosity.

"Eavl is the Nwyllan who has been here all the time," Ufd went on. "I'm Ufd—or Eldin Raigmore." He blocked the surge of disbelief and horror that came from Alison and went on hurriedly: "I'll explain later. There's a lot you and I have to do, but we can't start until Eavl is satisfied. Run through the tests as quickly as you can. It'll do no harm—and it may even help."

He was taking a lot for granted. Now that she knew who he was, though not whether he had always been a Nwyllan or just since their capture, she might refuse to co-operate, might even do her best to tell Eavl that Ufd was a traitor to both sides. But it was a small risk. Between half human and alien she was bound to choose the half human.

"You can break down now," he told Alison. "Eavl won't find it strange."

It was curious that the Nwyllans, the masters of deception, were so easy to deceive. Alison waited until the room was a furnace again, then suddenly burst into tears and turned quickly to the pattern test. Eavl stabilized the temperature, and in ten seconds Alison had completed the test.

She went on co-operating. The Terran Tests took weeks; Alison was through with the Nwyllan tests in less than four hours.

chapter eight

"CERTAINLY YOU CAN RETURN US WITHOUT ENDANGERING the plan," Ufd told Eavl. "It would be more difficult for me to cover the disappearance of Alison than to work on its mind and remove all knowledge of what has happened." That was impossible, but Eavl had no means of knowing it.

So as dawn broke on Earth, Alison and Raigmore were back in their bedroom, and the tiny shell which had landed them was on its way back to the huge Nwyllan ship.

"It's safe to talk now," said Raigmore.

"I don't want to talk," said Alison bitterly. "Who and what are you anyway?"

"I was a Nwyllan. I am Eldin Raigmore."

"We're sold, then, all Earth. The thing I married . . ." She shuddered.

"It's Nwylla I'm selling," said Raigmore.

That stopped her, as he had known it would. "Let's go and see Margo," he said.

"Margo! Then she's . . ."

"Listen, Alison. You know why I was put here. You know more than I did last night—a lot more. Last night I was waiting. And for weeks before that. I didn't know where I stood. Now I do. With my memories of Earth and Nwylla, I'm fighting for Earth. Is that so surprising?"

"Where, if that's so, did the Nwyllans make the mistake that puts you on our side?" she asked bluntly.

"I'm not certain, but I think it was in giving me a human body. And human knowledge, without any Nwyllan knowledge to direct it. When I first spoke to you, I was nine-tenths Nwyllan, though in a human body. But when you saw me In Test, I was already more than half human. Now . . ."

"How much now?"

"Practically all. I want to be human. I've seen both sides and made my choice. The thing is, I was more human than Nwyllan, even as Ufd."

He went on talking as they dressed. Characteristically, she was collecting evidence, not committing herself. But he could see that already, if the question of whether she believed him had to be answered yes or no, it would be answered yes.

Casually, impersonally, he told her that any children of a human and a Nwyllan in a human body would be completely human. He didn't apply it to himself and her, but he knew that, like any female, she must naturally have been thinking about that. She didn't say anything about it, but he felt her believing him, accepting him again, relaxing.

"You're a telepath," she said abruptly. "Can't you——"

"Not as a human. I'm pretty certain that with the double knowledge I have now I can make telepathy possible for humans. But not at once. Not in time to affect this problem."

"If all you say is true, the Nwyllans have won every time, and I can't see what's going to stop them now."

"That's how they win. Why attack Mars at all, except as a demonstration? Obviously, if it were possible—or rather, to the Nwyllan mind, if it were certain—it would be far better to overcome Earth in the first attack instead of wasting the element of surprise on Mars.

"The real question is how many of the Nwyllan agents here feel as I do."

Alison brightened at that. "Surely it must be all or none? If you've been converted to the Terran way of life, the Terran love of freedom, all the others must feel the same."

"Remember Mars?" said Raigmore wryly. He buttoned her dress at the back, and she didn't shrink from him. "The Nwyllans there have not only done their job, but are returned to their own bodies by this time and apparently without any question of changed loyalty. Otherwise the question would have come up in my case."

"I see. That's why we're going to see Margo."

It was too early for Margo to be up, but they waited until she came to the door of her bedroom in another part of the administration building. As she blinked at them, still heavy with sleep, Raigmore told her: "Go and have a cold shower first, Margo. You'll need it."

She went docilely, but Raigmore inclined his head for Alison to go with her. He wasn't quite certain about Margo.

She still hadn't told him about her private agent; Raigmore was certain she had one.

They were back in a few minutes, Margo wearing a wrap and fully awake. Raigmore told her what had happened, what he had discovered. He said nothing about what he had decided.

"Earth, of course," said Margo. "But what can we *do?*"

They didn't accept her just like that. But Raigmore saw Alison looking relieved. If the Nwyllan agents were all converts, the attack was going to fail.

She could test Margo for herself in a way she couldn't use with Raigmore. He watched her do it. He was Alison's equal, and if he wanted to lie to her she couldn't penetrate the deception. Margo wasn't her equal.

The way Margo relaxed when she began to understand was the most convincing thing of all. "I don't mind how bad it is," she said, "it's better than not knowing at all."

And at once, unprompted, she told Raigmore about the operative known only to her.

They brought Salter and Gloria in on it, and they all breakfasted together. It wasn't so easy to convince them as it had been with Alison, but it only took longer. It wasn't impossible. Raigmore reminded them that the P-ray Test had passed Margo and him.

"But how far is this to go?" Salter asked. "Nobody else that I can think of is going to say to you two, 'So you're Nwyllans, are you? Pleased to meet you.' Not Morton, certainly."

They talked it over, and agreed to modify the story for

others. They would say that Raigmore and Alison had been in contact with the Nwyllans, and leave it at that. Only the fact that Raigmore had been Ufd would be omitted.

"You carry on with that, Alison," said Raigmore. "The rest of us will go back to Millo and see the Nwyllans we know."

A helicopter piloted by Salter took them to Millo in half an hour. Raigmore and Salter called on Fenton first. The interview was wholly inconclusive. Nwyllan or no, Fenton was a Brown. He didn't have the intelligence to see the issues and work out a plan. All he could do was repeat patiently, over and over, that he didn't know what they were talking about.

He was turned over to a panel of psychologists, though Raigmore was certain that nothing could be learned from him. The psychologists were warned that he might insist that Raigmore was some kind of alien. They nodded. They had met this kind of delusion before.

They went next to see Carter. Despite their care, the Black guessed the real issue long before he was supposed to—and made a very determined and very nearly effective attempt to kill Raigmore.

Salter kicked his legs from under him, but even as he went down he shot at Raigmore. Raigmore, however, took care not to be where the bullet went, and Salter didn't allow Carter a second shot.

"He'll do his best to make the psychiatrists believe you're a spy," Salter murmured, as they prodded Carter in front of them out onto the landing and downstairs. "And he's smarter than Fenton. They may——"

But Carter solved that problem for them. He leaped forward, turning in the air. He fell to the next landing without touching any of the fourteen steps in between, and landed on the back of his head. The crack seemed as loud as the shot a few seconds before. He didn't even twitch.

Gloria and Margo, who had been left outside, came running upstairs, drawn by the sound of the shot. They almost tripped over Carter's body. They stared down at it, horrified. Suicide was almost unheard of, these days.

"Why should he do that?" Gloria muttered.

"He must have known something," said Raigmore. "We were careless. I was sure he didn't, or we wouldn't have given him the chance to kill himself. We must be much more careful with the other two."

The two who remained were Purples, and might easily be dangerous. "Peach first," said Raigmore. "The way she reacts should show us how to handle Herman."

They left Gloria to wait for the police.

They had to hurry to catch Peach before she went to work. In fact, they saw her in the street. Before she saw them, Salter dropped back. She wouldn't be suspicious at the sight of Raigmore and Margo together, but the presence of Salter with them might alert her.

Peach was entirely calm and reasonable. She saw the issues. She wasn't emotionally involved. Where did she stand? She simply didn't know.

Raigmore motioned to Salter, and he joined them.

"If Earth is going to win," said Peach frankly, "I'm with Earth."

"But if you saw any chance for Nwylla, you'd switch again?"

She didn't answer that. They were still watching her closely. Raigmore asked if she had any objection to being turned over to the psychiatric bureau.

"No," she said. "I can't help that, can I? If you do that, it'll remove responsibility from me."

Salter phoned the Depot, and they waited until a car arrived for her. They asked her, as a matter of course, if she knew of any other Nwyllan agents. She didn't.

"Which will be the truth," said Raigmore, as they watched the car taking her away. "This group is a closed circuit. I had a man Margo didn't know, and she had Herman. None of the others could give orders to anyone, for they weren't responsible. See how Peach was glad to give up all responsibility?"

Herman was going to be the most difficult to handle, since Raigmore wasn't supposed to know about him. If Raigmore appeared with Margo that might in itself be a signal for attack or suicide. Raigmore looked at Margo thoughtfully.

"How are you on responsibility, Margo?" he asked.

"I don't know what you mean."

"You have to see Herman alone, at first. He may try to kill you. Do you want to die?"

"That's nonsense," she said impatiently.

They were still standing out in the street, Salter looking curiously from Margo to Raigmore and back.

"Wouldn't it be nice if you could get out of this altogether by being dead, like Carter, and not having to think or make decisions or fight against Nwylla or——"

She burst into tears. They took her into a café and ordered coffee. "Go on," said Raigmore sympathetically. "Cry all you like."

"You think I'm weak."

"Of course you're weak. So was I, or I'd have gone on working for Nwylla. I didn't like killing people, I didn't like Hever being murdered. I didn't like the idea of Earth as a Nwyllan colony. In this company you can be weak if you like."

The girl who brought the coffee couldn't help staring at Margo.

"She doesn't know which of us she loves best," Salter told her cheerfully. "If she takes one, she loses the other. Just look at us. Wouldn't you cry too?"

The girl had another look at them. Only one badge on display among them, and that a Red Star. She beat a hasty retreat, wondering, perhaps, what a Red Star who looked like that, with two men like that, could possibly have to cry about.

Margo gradually stopped crying. "That's the first time I've ever done that," she said. "You know, there's something rather pleasant about it."

"I've always thought so," said Salter. "Some girls do it most of the time."

"I'm glad you said that," Margo told Raigmore. "I don't know what I'd have done—I don't think I'd have let Herman kill me, if he tried that. But perhaps . . ."

"Perhaps you'd have run unnecessary risks," said Raigmore. "That's a human characteristic. So's crying to relieve your feelings. You're no Nwyllan, Margo. You're a human girl, and quite emotional at that."

"Are the Nwyllans bisexual?" Salter asked.

"No. There's only one sex. Margo might have been a man."

Salter shuddered. "I like her much better as she is. And as for you, if you'd been a girl Alison wouldn't have got much fun out of it."

chapter nine

THE BEST PLAN SEEMED TO BE TO GET HERMAN TO GO TO Margo's flat, where Raigmore and Salter could wait out of sight. Salter had kept Carter's gun. While they were waiting for him, Salter glanced quizzically at Raigmore.

"You were just talking about feeling," he said, "as if you knew what it meant. But isn't it a bit ruthless to betray members of your own race to another? And it doesn't seem to worry you at all."

"It doesn't worry me," Raigmore told him. "There's no affection among Nwyllans. When Nwyllans agree and work together, it's because it's to the advantage of both of them. Immediately it's no longer to the advantage of one, they both take it for granted the partnership's over. The only disagreement that can occur is when two people calculate on the same basis and come to different conclusions.

They're certainly much more reasonable than Terrans."

He shrugged his shoulders. "Of course I betray Nwyllans. Both as a human and as a Nwyllan I can't see anything else it's possible to do. And as for ruthlessness—the question doesn't arise when you're dealing with Nwyllans. They're no more ruthless than they are kindhearted."

They were silent then, in case Herman heard their voices from outside.

When he came, Margo gave him a chair so that Raigmore and Salter were both behind him. She put the issue to him calmly, and he took it much as Peach had done. She looked up to invite Raigmore and Salter to come out.

Herman interpreted the movement correctly. In one movement he hit her in the stomach, grasped a handful of the material of her skirt and dragged her in front of him. He was shooting at Raigmore when he first saw him. Margo was too dazed to do anything, the breath knocked out of her.

Salter put a bullet in Herman's wrist, but instantly Herman took the gun in his left hand and crushed Margo against him with his injured right arm. He shot at Salter and Salter's gun dropped. Raigmore dived for it and shot Herman from the floor, through Margo's legs. Even then, as Herman fell, he had strength left for a shot at Margo. Raigmore shot again.

"For heaven's sake!" said Salter, as the echoes died. "Such malevolence! Such determination!" He took two quick steps and caught Margo as she fell.

They looked at Margo first, though Salter noticed Raigmore was hopping awkwardly. The bullet had gone through her side, above the waist. Salter probed with his fingers. "Between the ribs, apparently," he said. "See if you can find some—no, you can't, can you. I'll do it."

He found bandages himself, pulled Margo's blouse out of her skirt and stopped the bleeding. "Nothing in that," he said. "Two days in bed. Now how about you?"

"We might need him," said Raigmore, nodding down at Herman.

"We'll need you more, more's the pity. But as you say."

Herman's right wrist was shattered, and Raigmore's first shot had struck the thighbone. The second creased him neatly, along the top of the head.

"He's all right," said Salter.

"Phone the police, then."

"We should have gone round calling this morning," Salter observed, "with the entire Millo police force and psychiatric bureau in procession with lots of ambulances. Yes, it's us again," he said into the phone. "Two ambulance cases, one of them for the psychiatric bureau. I'm sorry, but people will keep getting in the way whenever we shoot a gun."

Margo tried to sit up. "Stay where you are," Salter told her. "I think it's only a flesh wound, but I haven't had much experience of this sort of thing. Haven't known you and Raigmore long. Don't worry about that blood on your skirt. It isn't yours."

He turned his attention to Raigmore, and found a bullet had taken a piece out of his calf. "Is that all?" he said disgustedly. "And here you've been pretending to be gravely wounded."

Raigmore leaned on Salter and laughed weakly, partly in reaction. "While you were the real hero," he said. "Why did you drop that gun? Give me those bandages."

He cut up Salter's sleeve and attended to the flesh wound on his forearm. "Yes, it's been quite a party," he said more soberly. "Well, let's remember there are fifty thousand Nwyllan-humans like Fenton and Carter and Herman around. If many of them are like Herman you can guess what we're up against. And I should say most of them are."

chapter ten

MARGO WENT TO THE HOSPITAL BUT WOULDN'T STAY. WITH Salter she was given the job of organizing Earth's defenses on lines that Raigmore laid down. Unlike her, he had his Nwyllan and Terran knowledge.

"Unfortunately I'm not a scientist," he said. "I know what most of the Nwyllan weapons will do, but not what makes them do it." Nevertheless, he could work out what Terran weapons would be effective and which wouldn't, and the general lines of successful defense. He knew how the rapidly growing fleet should be equipped, and what sort of men should be its officers.

The real problem was to cut out sabotage. It appeared that anyone who came out high in the Tests was, among other things, all for the system which produced them. All for Earth's way of life. It was to be expected that the others among the fifty thousand who rated high would agree with Raigmore and Margo, given the opportunity.

There was the rub. Raigmore himself was uncertain whether he would have changed sides unreservedly if there had been no further contact to give him back his Nwyllan knowledge. Others, like Margo, would go on acting as they were supposed to act until they were given a lead.

But there was one obvious safety step—all defenses to be taken over by Reds or higher. That would either cut out Nwyllans altogether or ensure fundamental sympathy with the ideals of Earth in those who controlled the defense setup.

"Just one little thing," Salter interposed at this point. "Where are you going to get all the Reds?"

Alison worked on that problem. The Whites were called in, of course, which theoretically meant a tremendous increase in potential. She worked on a principle of replacing three Reds with an Orange, passing on the work of several Oranges to a Yellow, and setting one White to the jobs vacated by several Yellows. That released enough Reds for the job.

When the take-over started, Margo very shortly had another job.

In those first few hours three Reds were killed and a lot of other attempts were frustrated.

It had not been openly stated there there were fifty thousand saboteurs on Earth. That was a secret which trickled down from the top. These murders and the attempted murders really awoke the public to the danger. They knew about Mars, they knew Earth would soon have to defend herself. But until then they had thought of Earth as a great, united front.

Margo was sent round to interview not only the people who had killed or tried to kill the Reds but the Reds concerned.

"We know from the case of Carter and Herman," said Raigmore, "that the top Nwyllan saboteurs are watched by someone who has the job of liquidating them if necessary. I don't quite know what's happened in these cases, but it looks as if the Reds concerned have made it clear that they really meant to defend Earth. So it became the job of the Carters and Hermans to destroy them."

It had to be Margo, for only she could be reasonably certain that she could identify the Nwyllans. She and Raigmore, and Raigmore was too busy.

Nothing was ever learned from any Nwyllan who was handed over to the psychiatric bureau. Nothing, at any rate, that wasn't already known or guessed.

Some of the saboteurs had fairly detailed instructions, involving considerable knowledge of their purpose. Those who guarded Nwyllan Reds were in this category. Others knew nothing except that they must conceal the fact that they had no knowledge of an existence before a few months ago, and that when Earth's safety depended on them they must contrive to fail. Their talents were always such that they would inevitably, through the Tests system, be drafted to some such job.

Margo called on Raigmore during a flying visit to Millo. "I wanted to show you these and see if you could improve on them," she said.

She was showing some sign of strain. She seemed to feel that she had to work much harder against the Nwyllans than the humans, as a sort of penance for once having been a Nwyllan herself. And Reds didn't have the stability of the Yellows, like Gloria and Salter, and the Whites.

Raigmore examined the papers she put in front of him. He saw they were tests designed to separate Nwyllans from ordinary humans.

"I must have been one of the first to be landed," she said. "That was just over a year ago. So the first thing is to find when the person concerned started In Test."

Raigmore nodded.

"That's not as helpful as you might think," Margo observed. "The usual time for Tests is between twenty and twenty-five. Most of the saboteurs are between twenty and twenty-five. And all these drafted to defense at the beginning of the emergency were in the same limits."

"So there's a big proportion of the defense force, anyway, who started In Test during the last year?"

"Yes. Point two—few of the Nwyllans have married. Naturally, though they played their parts well, they tended to be pretty cold and humorless, at least at first, and nobody either liked them much or disliked them. That's point three —a Nwyllan tends to have no friends and no enemies. Or if he has, they've become friends or enemies fairly recently. Point four—none so far discovered had any physical defects. That part of the Nwyllan job was done a little too well."

Raigmore looked at her thoughtfully. "That should pretty well sew it up," he observed.

"Yes, if we're given enough time. We remove from positions of trust all people between twenty and twenty-five who started In Test less than a year ago and draft in anyone, anyone at all, who started before that. We also tend to prefer married people, people who are popular or unpopular, who have a sense of humor, who are emotional, and who have or had some physical defect. Once we've done that there won't be many Nwyllans left."

She was right; but the process of replacement had hardly been started when the Nwyllan fleet left Mars and attacked.

chapter eleven

THE NWYLLANS, DESPITE THE FACT THAT THEY THOUGHT SO differently from Terrans, had a certain knowledge of psychology which was probably fundamental, common to all races that thought.

They massed clear of Mars, the whole thousand of them, quite openly, inviting the people of Earth to remember the fate of Mars and to set up their various defense fields around Earth, if they thought it would do any good. Then, in wide formation, they started to Earth at about four times the acceleration the human body could stand. Halfway between planets—the distance at the time was about seventy million miles—they went right over from acceleration to deceleration.

The communications room in Washington in which Raigmore, Gloria and Margo waited for the first reports to come in was normally part of the education department. It was large and circular, and all the way round the walls was a giant map of the world. It started three feet from the floor and extended right to the ceiling high above. Below the map were racks filled with long pointers which could be used to place magnetized flags anywhere on the metal surface of the map.

Raigmore and the two girls stood in the little railed dais in the middle, waiting. Scores of men and women stood around the walls, also waiting. In appearance they were a motley crew. Most of them were government clerks, stenographers, administrators. But there were also police chiefs, statisticians, space-navy men, senators and Tests operators. There were elderly men in formal clothes and girls of seventeen in shorts, people who held themselves stiffly and youngsters who lounged and laughed and whispered, grim people and excited people. There were people who were there because they were important in the defense setup of Earth, because Raigmore might need them, and there were people recruited merely to put flags where they were told to put them on the map.

Margo was responsible for the system of flags. "The green flags," she explained, "mean the personnel there has been checked—it's reasonably certain there are no Nwyllans. The red, orange, yellow and white flags mean there's been no efficient check, but there's a Red or higher in charge there. The blacks are the doubtful points, neither checked nor controlled by a Red."

"I thought we had Reds everywhere," said Gloria, who hadn't been concerned in this part of the organization.

"In over-all command, yes. But we haven't Reds for every defense point."

Raigmore was frowning at a hastily prepared sheet which gave the disposition of the space navy. There was a regular fleet, maintained at all times, but it was small. Morton had expanded it all it could efficiently be expanded in the time they had had; but Raigmore knew that if the two fleets, Nwyllan and Terran, met in space the Earth fleet would be routed in a matter of seconds. There was no question of engaging the Nwyllans in space. A fleet couldn't be trained in a few days.

Yet Raigmore knew that the space navy, used near the surface as a sort of super air force, was all he had in reserve. Ordinary planes were useless against space ships; only other space ships might accomplish anything against them. And if extra force was needed anywhere, all Raigmore could do was send a few ships of Earth's infant navy to see what they could do to help.

"We've only identified about five hundred probable Nwyllans," Margo was saying.

"Five hundred, of fifty thousand!" exclaimed Gloria. "That means——"

They soon saw what it meant.

Alison herself was in charge of the Washington defenses, with Salter to help her. So in Washington there was never any actual, visible attack as there was in so many other places. Alison and Salter dealt with any sign of sabotage before it made any serious difference. In the communications room Raigmore and Margo could forget about the defense of Washington and concentrate on the general position shown on the map.

The first attack was on Europe, but that, it seemed, was a diversion. No European city fell; one Nwyllan ship was destroyed, that was all.

"But they must know already from that," Gloria remarked, "that we know more than Mars did. No one in London or Berlin opened the door for them."

"Perhaps there was no one in London or Berlin to open it," said Raigmore soberly. "We may have the whole fifty thousand here."

In any case, the full, all-out attack was on North America. Fifteen seconds after the first attack was registered on New York, the room was in uproar, scores of men and women milling about the map to register other attacks.

But soon a pattern began to emerge. The Nwyllan ships, darting about at speeds no ship manned by humans could hope to match, were touching check points one after another, testing their reception.

Raigmore ordered the entire Terran fleet out of the air. The Nwyllans were so superior in maneuverability that the losses the human fleet must be suffering, though there was no data yet, would be out of all proportion to their destructive effect.

Defense points began to go down. Blue domes—meaning either the end of all communication or a Nwyllan ship through all defenses, unharmed—were placed over spots on the map—two in Kansas, three in Alaska, one over Winnipeg, others in California, Iowa, Michigan and Oklahoma.

No domes went over green flags; only a few over red and orange flags.

"Fifteen—sixteen," exclaimed Margo. "Seventeen—why didn't we get around more? We did so little when we had time——"

"We did all we could," said Raigmore quietly.

There were few orders he could give. Both the Nwyllan and the Terran forces were operating on orders given in advance. Now all that Raigmore could do was watch what happened.

Everyone paused for a moment as someone set up a figure above the map. It was 31—the number of Nwyllan ships destroyed or disabled. Two girls cheered shrilly. But by this time there more than thirty blue domes on the map.

Raigmore read a few of the reports which came in from some of the blue-dome sectors. In each case the Nwyllan ship—it was never more than one—got through the defense screens unharmed, and in each case it was suggested that the coverage had been faulty. The reports usually stopped there. But sometimes they went on to describe what the Nwyllan beams were doing. When they did, it was always the same story of power, death and ruin. The Nwyllan purpose meantime seemed to be nothing but destruction—the greatest possible destruction in the shortest time.

There was a moment's hush in the buzz of the communications room as a dome was placed over Philadelphia. That was the first time a green flag had been covered. It was also the first really serious loss. Almost at once domes were placed in New York State and over Baltimore. Both covered green flags.

At the same time the figure of Nwyllan ships destroyed was changed to 35. No one cheered this time. They had thought it would be at least seventy.

Raigmore sent ten ships of the grounded Terran fleet to Baltimore, with orders to move in, concentrating on their own defense at first rather than attack.

At his shoulder Margo spoke with an intensity which surprised him: "None of us with any feeling at all will be in any doubt now. This tells us all what side we're on."

A message came from Alison. She wanted ships if Raigmore could spare them. It was the first indication that the battle was going on over their heads as well as everywhere else. Raigmore transferred ten ships to her—only ten, for Washington wasn't of supreme importance. If ten weren't enough to sway the balance, he saw no reason to commit more.

"Ninety-seven domes," said Margo. There was blood on her hands, Raigmore noticed. She hadn't noticed her nails digging into her plams. Gently he took her hand in his and unclenched it.

He sent Gloria to get a more detailed picture from Alison, or to see for herself what was going on if Alison was too busy to tell her. There would certainly be a heavy attack on Washington; Alison must have learned a lot.

The figure above the map was changed to 39. No spectacular success could be expected there.

There was a more general cheer as the dome was taken off Baltimore. Though the officer only removed it to put it back over Charleston, it was the first time defeat was shown not to be irrevocable and that a Nwyllan ship, through the defenses, could still be destroyed. As the figure 39 was altered to 40 there was even some nervous laughter.

"A hundred and seven," Margo muttered.

Raigmore realized with some confusion that in the moment of crisis he had become largely Nwyllan again. His emotions weren't involved; he was as cool as if he were playing a game of chess.

Gloria came dashing back, skirt flying. It was the first time Raigmore had seen her upset and out of breath.

"Alison's holding off a hundred ships," she gasped. "She needs anything more you can spare. Otherwise Washington will go down, and all of us with it."

chapter twelve

IF WASHINGTON WAS IMPORTANT ENOUGH TO THE NWYLLANS for them to throw in a tenth of their force, it was worth as much to Earth to keep them out. Raigmore detailed twenty-five more ships to join the Washington defense force.

"Wait!" he exclaimed as Gloria started to hurry back. "Margo, you go. Stay with Alison and help."

He caught Gloria as she moved again in defiance of his command. His arm round her waist, he was surprised, even at such a moment, to find how vibrant and attractive the rather austere Gloria was in his grasp.

"Wait till you get your breath back," he said. "People dashing about breathless aren't good for morale—especially people like you. See what this means? They know I at least have changed sides, and probably more of us. They're trying to eliminate me. But I'm not as important as they think, now that Earth's organized for defense against them. Tell Alison we're not holding Washington at all costs. If it's going to fall, get the ships out."

Still he didn't let her go. The number of Nwyllan ships accounted for went up to 49.

"Tell Alison we're doing well," he said.

"Are we?"

There were a hundred and fourteen blue domes on the map now.

"Yes," he said, and released her. She didn't run, remembering what he had said about morale.

More domes were coming off now, if only to be replaced somewhere else. Raigmore recalled what he knew of other Nwyllan campaigns. He was glad he had never taken part in any of them—he had been too young, and had been bred purely for the Terran campaign. No other race had put up a defense anything like this. Even if Earth went down, the conquest would have a lot of question marks after it in the Nwyllan calendar.

In the communications room everything was done in silence now. It was obvious there was going to be no sudden swing one way or the other. This could be victory or defeat, but nothing was going to happen at once.

Morton appeared rather apologetically and handed Raigmore a sheet of paper. It was an estimate of the loss in human lives since the attack started.

Raigmore tried to balance it and tell himself that the

figures before him represented a resounding victory. But he had a terrifying glimpse of the horror of this kind of battle, where in minutes more lives could be extinguished than whole wars of Earth's past had destroyed. Every unit in the total before him represented a man or woman who had seen that day dawn and would never see another.

Nwyllan ships destroyed—56. Only fifty-six Nwyllans to balance the sickening figures in front of him.

A new front opened. The Nwyllans, as if contemptuous of all that North America could do, returned to the assault on Europe. The first blue dome was clapped over England —Southampton. Another over Middlesbrough. Two in southern France. One in Italy; Rome had fallen yet again to another conqueror.

Raigmore crumpled the paper in his hand and tried to think as a Nwyllan again. The Nwyllans were mathematicians. As long as it seemed a mathematical certainty that the last Nwyllan ship would be left master of Earth, they would go on. But whenever it was obvious, however small their losses, that there could be no victory, they would withdraw.

Salter rushed in. "You crazy fool!" he bellowed at Raigmore. "You're the only decisive weapon we've got against the Nwyllans. If you're lost, what can Earth do?"

"I make no difference," Raigmore told him. "I've passed on all I can."

"You confounded Nwyllan, Raigmore," Salter exclaimed, "can't you see you're more than just a leader, more than a textbook on Nwyllan tactics? Stop thinking like a calculating machine and try to work out what Eldin Raigmore, White Star, means to Earth and the people in it!

They love you, the stupid fools. I know they've no reason, they don't know you, they may hate you tomorrow—but they rely on you, and if you're not around they'll think it's all over."

Raigmore regarded him thoughtfully. Salter was the best friend he had, the only friend he had, not counting the three women and possibly Sally Morris. But there was no sign of friendliness about him at the moment.

Another Nwyllan would be in charge of the attacking forces, but he didn't matter to the Nwyllans under him. If he was destroyed, it meant merely the elimination of one unit, and another Nwyllan immediately took over.

"We only have the fleet, Fred," he said quietly. "It wasn't a fighting force until a week or two ago. It can't even fly in formation, for it doesn't know how. And when it's gone, there's nothing more to throw in. We may have billions of people, but they can't fight the Nwyllans with wooden sticks."

Salter was silent, but his eyes didn't drop from Raigmore's.

"I'll order fifty ships from Pittsburgh," said Raigmore, "but that's all I can do. I'll commit everything, since if we're beaten everything's lost anyway."

He gave the orders. Salter left him, paused at the door, shook his head and went out.

Raigmore ordered attack everywhere, even at the expense of defense. The Nwyllans would not be concerned at all about the damage they did; it was the shape of the battle that would exercise them. If they could be shown a mathematical certainty of defeat, they would go.

The blue dome had disappeared from Southampton. As Raigmore looked at the map again, the dome was removed from Middlesbrough too. The British fleet was still almost whole. In Europe there could be a concentration of force which wasn't possible in America.

Nwyllans down—71. Domes—129.

The effect of the change in orders began to be apparent. Domes disappeared and the total of Nwyllan casualties mounted. But Raigmore waved Morton away when he came with another slip of paper. His order must already have sent Earth's losses rocketing. This was self-defense—the loss of life had ceased to have any meaning.

There was a pause. Raigmore felt it as if two teams, hard at it, had stopped for a break to gather their forces for a final all-out effort.

The officer in charge apologetically took down 93 as the figure of Nwyllan losses and put up 92. But then blue domes were coming off, first here and there, then in big areas, then from all over the map. Raigmore relaxed, and instantly felt agony in all parts of his body. Like Margo, he hadn't known what he was doing to himself.

The domes couldn't be taken off fast enough. One jubilant officer swept off half a dozen with one sweep of his arm. They clattered on the floor and swung on their tops like pendulums.

Raigmore had shown the Nwyllan commander his mathematical certainty.

chapter thirteen

MOST OF EARTH WAS WILDLY JUBILANT AS THE LAST OF THE invaders disappeared. If they had known the whole story, that it was one of the very few times that the Nwyllans had been beaten off in this way, they would have been even more confident. Nearly everyone regarded the fight as over.

"Which, I'm afraid, is nonsense," said Raigmore at the security council meeting he convened immediately. "We've done as we hoped we'd do—not quite as well as I thought we might."

This council was more sober than the public. There were no protests at his warning, except from Salter.

"Cheer up," he said, "we might have been pushed into the sun. These Nwyllans have gone away with their tails between their legs—surely that's a good start?"

Most of the information Raigmore could give had been handed out openly. His story, which was in fair accord with the Nwyllans' methods, was that they had told him frankly all that he passed on. All Earth knew she was fighting Nwylla. That helped. An enemy whose very name was unknown would have been much more terrible.

But Raigmore's fiction couldn't last. One couldn't go on deceiving Whites as more and more facts were presented to them.

"It won't be victory for Earth merely to drive the Nwyllans off," Raigmore declared. "Already, almost certainly, a complete picture of the situation must be on the way to Nwylla itself. Earth can be flooded with Nwyllans. Occasionally, before, that technique has been necessary."

Alison, at his side, caught his arm. Salter and Gloria turned, startled; Margo wasn't there. In the gathering there was a sudden roar as everyone there realized, not what was going on, but that *something* was going on. And there was equally sudden silence as Raigmore spoke again.

"Maier," he said, "you were right at the first meeting. Earth is full of spies. Some of you know that. Some of you only know we've been replacing the defense personnel. . . . Nwylla, by means I can't tell you here and now, can plant as many spies among us as she needs. There were fifty thousand. Now—we don't know. I think we've broken them. Thousands are dead and we have identified and captured most of the rest. We can complete the process now. But the Nwyllans can land more——"

It was too much to give them all at once. There hadn't been time yet even to reckon the cost of the battle, to sift all the information and discover exactly what had happened. It was too soon. . . . Momentarily even these people, the leaders of Earth, hated Raigmore for reminding them that the fight was anything but over, and introducing things they didn't know and showing them they couldn't rest to lick their wounds.

They didn't want to believe him, so they didn't. They shouted and jumped up and some of them denied that there were any spies at all, trying to stop Raigmore telling them what they might have to admit was true.

"There *were* fifty thousand Nwyllans among us," said Alison, so quietly that they had to quiet to hear her. "Those of you who know anything about this had better confirm that to the others before we go on, for that's nothing to what I think you're going to hear in a moment."

She sat down again and whispered to Raigmore: "Are you sure you're right to tell them? Suppose they——"

"I must," Raigmore murmured. "We've shown that fifty thousand Nwyllans and a thousand ships aren't enough to conquer Earth. The Nwyllans will accept that, and try . . . oh, the numbers I could give you are too big to mean anything. So . . ."

He turned to Salter. "Fred," he said, "I doubt if they'd find it possible to believe me. Will you tell them?"

"No," said Alison. "If you must, Eldin. tell them yourself. It would be better."

Raigmore nodded. She would know.

He told them who and what he was.

They didn't understand at first. If Raigmore was a Nwyllan, why should he tell them? But it was impossible—he couldn't be a Nwyllan. He was a White Star, and he had beaten the Nwyllans. He had told them what to do, and he had done the rest himself. Everyone there knew that but for Raigmore Earth would have been defeated already. He had done an enormous job, taken an enormous responsibility— one man, even Raigmore, might easily have become unbalanced under the strain. That must be what had happened.

Alison spoke again. She didn't raise her voice, and everyone lost her first words. ". . . but I'm no Nwyllan, you know that. Obviously Raigmore wouldn't have said this if he weren't unreservedly for us. And I'm his wife—think about that."

They thought about that, wonderingly. Alison went on: "We needn't talk about that. What I want to know is what he's going to do. Whatever it is, I'm with him. How about you? Remember, Raigmore is still our main hope. I'd say that if I hated him, instead of . . ."

She couldn't talk about love before a gathering like that. But they understood. She had brought them together again. There was utter silence as Raigmore told them simply and frankly the only thing he could see to do now.

chapter fourteen

THE COUNCIL WAS GONE. IT WASN'T A MATTER FOR COUNCILS any more. The five people who were there were close friends, if they were also five of the most important people on Earth. They stood in the council chamber and argued as friends, not councilors.

Margo was almost crying. "It can't be you, Raigmore," she said passionately. "Do you think the Nwyllans would let you come back afterward? They'd be fools if they did. Let me go—you can instruct me if you like, tell me what to say."

She caught his arm tightly. "Don't tell me I won't put the case as well as you. I know that. It won't surprise them either. And if I can't put it as well, I'll put it as strongly——"

"I want Margo here," said Salter. "I love her, Raigmore, Nwyllan or not, and I think she'd love me in the end. But she's right. Remember what I said to you in the communications room? It's still true, all of it. If you put yourself in the Nwyllans' power, they'll simply destroy you and come back to destroy Earth. It has to be you or Margo, since you're the only two we can trust, even as Nwyllans, and if it's you we're losing more than we can possibly gain."

Raigmore smiled wryly. "I wish you people would be yourselves," he said. "Here's Fred talking as if he hadn't a grain of humor in him and Margo acting like a Nwyllan."

"Like a Nwyllan?" Margo exclaimed.

Raigmore got up. "The rest of you wait here," he said. "I'm going to shake some sense into Margo. If you hear any screams, just ignore them. It's for her own good."

He took Margo's arm and marched her into a little room off the chamber. He put his hands on her shoulders and looked down into her eyes.

"Remember when you wanted Herman to kill you, Margo?" he asked quietly.

She flushed. "I didn't——"

"I know. You just wanted to be out of the way. I've got my Nwyllan memories, Margo, and you haven't. And wanting to be out of the way like that is a Nwyllan characteristic, about the only one I've seen in you. When things get too tough for them, or when there's no longer any chance of promoting Empire, they just stop. That's all—stop. Sometimes it means dying, sometimes they go on existing for a while.

"You wanted me, and you can't have me. You've stopped

working for Empire, long ago. You've got nothing to live for, have you?"

"Of course I've got something to——"

In contrast with the gentleness of his manner and expression, Raigmore shook her. She protested, then laughed, then protested again as the shaking became more severe.

Raigmore let her go. "You haven't looked into this, that's the trouble," he told her. "Well, look into it now."

He took a big clasp knife from his pocket, snapped it open, and put the point on her breast. "That's very sharp," he said, "and four inches long. You'd hardly feel it." He took her hand and clasped it over the hilt of the knife. "If you want to die, see how easy it is? Just pull hard on that, and we won't be able to save you."

She stayed still for a long time, looking at him, not the knife. Then she took it away from her breast, snapped it shut and handed it back.

"Funny, I never thought of that being the easy way," she said. "All right, Raigmore. You've made your point. I want to live. But . . ."

She looked up at him sharply. "Do you? Or is it the same with you? Are you surrendering, giving yourself up, because you——"

"No," he said quietly. "It's because I want to live that I'm doing this. If I don't do it, Earth may still be destroyed —and me with Earth. Come on, let's go back."

Salter and Gloria were arguing with Alison. "Yes, Alison," said Raigmore, "I haven't heard your point of view. What is it?"

"You're right, Eldin," said Alison steadily, "and I haven't been able to make myself believe that you're not. You say the Nwyllans are an inherently reasonable people, and you should know. If you think by going out and talking to them you can convince them that conquest of Earth is meantime impossible, I suppose you have to do it."

"Thanks, Alison," said Raigmore quietly. "Frankly, I didn't care much whether the others saw that or not, so long as you did."

chapter fifteen

THE SINGLE TINY SHIP FLEW ON TOWARD MARS. MOST OF THE Terran fleet had accompanied it part of the way, merely as a gesture to the Nwyllans. Morton and a few others were afraid they would snuff it out without investigating it at all, but Raigmore told them that was out of the question. They would capture it and make sure it was secure, but they certainly wouldn't harm the being inside, whoever he might be, before trying to discover all they could.

"Anyway," he told them, "they'll know it's me. When the attack failed it would be obvious not merely that some of the saboteurs had changed sides but that I must be among them. They know the new factor, the unexpected factor: that Nwyllans can be traitors to Empire. They'll listen to me."

He didn't think, on the journey, of what he was going

to say. He thought of Earth, and all that had happened to him there. He thought of Alison.

Life among humans wasn't really as his, so far, had been. He had only had a few weeks of relaxation, and even that had been full of doubt, anxiety, indecision, waiting for something to happen. Too much had been going on practically all the time he was Eldin Raigmore. Human life was an affair of human relationships, affections, likes, dislikes, loves. He hoped he would have a chance to experience that kind of life, a chance to get to know people, lots of people.

There was a possibility that he would, he thought. He would have had to do this anyway; but, knowing the Nwyllans, he believed there was a chance.

They didn't know there was such a thing as revenge. That was his chance. They did inhuman things to people, to groups, to whole races—naturally, not being human— when these might act as warnings. That was *before* the event, to supply a motive. But *after* the event, once a thing was done, it wasn't reasonable to punish unless it could be a warning to others.

Revenge was human. It had no meaning for the Nwyllans.

Raigmore hadn't known it was possible to feel so utterly alone. He stood on his many legs among his own people, feeling like the last living thing in a dead galaxy.

The scene, the meeting place on one of the Nwyllan ships, would have bewildered human eyes. Fifty Nwyllans stood like so many trees on the green copper which was the normal flooring in Nwyllan ships. Comfort and softness are bound up with pleasure, and Nwyllans felt pleasure only in spreading Empire. A source of discomfort was only removed when the discomfort would interfere with the proper functioning of the Nwyllan concerned. Nothing but bare metal was to be seen, chiefly copper.

The scene could eventually be learned, made familiar. But no human, except Raigmore, would ever fully understand the conversation that ensued, even if it were translated for him and explained to him. A motive to a Nwyllan would not be a motive to a human. And a Nwyllan would accept as proof something a human would not have as a premise.

Raigmore didn't fight his loneliness as he stood there. He felt it as intensely as he could, broadcasting it with all his mental power. He felt barriers being erected hastily on all sides. The Nwyllans couldn't take that emotion.

Desolation isn't the pleasantest introduction to emotion.

Stop came a thought at him. It carried a lot of concepts with it—stop, cease, die, too much, never. He took them all, and as a further demonstration, loaded them with the appropriate emotion and sent them back.

"No more of this—say what you have to say," came in a thought which Raigmore recognized as from Eavl. "Or are you too mad to communicate without this . . ."

Blank. There was no concept.

To show he could do it, Raigmore shut off all emotion, completely, instantly.

"You know I am here voluntarily," he thought. "I came to tell you what is going to happen between Nwylla and Earth."

He thought with all the coldness of Ufd, but concealed

under it all the strength and determination of Raigmore, of Earth, of his human experience.

"My conversion to Earth was automatic," he declared, as point one.

He showed them the steps, logically. He couldn't tell them why it happened. They wouldn't have understood. But he could show them, nevertheless, that it must; Nwyllans differed hardly at all in character, only in capacity. If he and Margo had changed, all Nwyllans like them would change.

Where doubt remained, he showed more detail. Some of it wasn't true, or was given a false significance, but that wouldn't even occur to them as a possibility. He didn't present any argument which a Nwyllan couldn't accept.

Almost all of it was essentially true. He might change the premise "Some S is P" to "All S is P," and the Nwyllans, knowing that some S was P, would accept it.

He pointed out that if the Nwyllans flooded Earth with saboteurs—and that would be difficult, now that Earth was warned—all the top Nwyllans would join Earth, as he and Margo had done.

"They could be differently constructed," someone thought. "They could be trained to resist Terran ideas."

"Then they would be discovered immediately," Raigmore shot back. He showed them the Tests system in one indigestible lump. They believed him.

That was one thing about arguing with Nwyllans—you knew where you were. If Raigmore couldn't get them to agree, he could make sure that they didn't disagree, and could know that ground was covered.

He showed them a picture of further attack, more Nwyllans on Earth as humans; the average Nwyllan going on with his job, the above-average Nwyllan becoming a Terran.

"They would not allow it," came a thought. The concept "they" pointed to the humans. "They are too intelligent."

"They *have* allowed it," Raigmore pointed out. He showed how he had been accepted, how Margo had been accepted, how all the other Reds who had been Nwyllans would be accepted.

He went on painting his picture: the Nwyllan force stripped at the top, the best men converted to a new point of view, a new way of life. Nwylla's worst fighting for Nwylla, Nwylla's best fighting for Earth, for freedom; eventually, to free other worlds throughout the galaxy meantime under Nwylla. A new force in the galaxy—from the Nwyllan point of view, a cancer. And already a cancer which could not be cut out. This was not what *might* happen; it was what *must* happen, if the Nwyllans went on with their plans.

Raigmore made the points coldly, precisely and well. He didn't make all the points he could have made. He didn't explain that if the stronger, higher, more intelligent Nwyllans had a natural predilection for the Terran way of life, a natural bias toward it, it was inevitable that Nwyllan goals must gradually change.

The Nwyllans were such that they would tell the truth, seeing no possible danger in the truth. And the top Nwyllans would wonder, theorize, examine and test human ideals —and to some very limited extent accept them.

Imperceptibly, the Nwyllan goal would change. But that was for the future.

Time was nothing to Nwyllans, except when a battle was in progress. Raigmore must have stood there and argued for eight or nine hours. He proved over and over again that he was sane—that is, reasonable. The Nwyllans knew no other form of insanity.

They admitted gradually, point by point, what he wanted them to admit. They could, of course, stay on Mars until they were driven off; but Raigmore, showing them more and more of what human beings were like, made it clear that they would certainly be driven off, in time.

At last only one thing remained. They admitted the truth of what Raigmore said, but they could not permit him to return to Earth and assist the Terrans further. Logically, they must destroy him.

Raigmore didn't agree. Might they not at some time need rapid, comprehensive contact with Earth? Wasn't it unreasonable to destroy the possibility of such easy, immediate contact, when a later situation might be simplified if he, Raigmore, were available?

He won even that point.

Then for five hours more they went over the whole ground again, testing Raigmore's argument for flaws, checking it against all the independent data they had. If there were any, the Nwyllans failed to find them.

There weren't any, really. The Nwyllans would never beat the humans, now that they were warned.

chapter sixteen

COMING IN TO LAND AT WASHINGTON, RAIGMORE SAW THE crowds waiting to shout his name and cheer him. He saw them from miles up—a black, seething mass of humanity flowing into every open space. When he was still high above the field he saw the black mass become speckled with white as every face was turned up toward him.

Salter had been right when he said they loved him. They did love him, these Browns and Purples who were so much more representative of humanity than the Whites, Yellows and Reds among whom he had spent almost all his time as a man. They idolized him, and he didn't want to be idolized.

But at least, he thought, without really applying it to himself, people now idolized the men and women they *should* appreciate, the men and women who would know what to do with their appreciation—try to use it to make a better world. If idolatry still existed, the people to idolize were the White Stars. They were the people who were really working for the people.

Landing was a tricky business, for only a tiny space could be kept clear for him. They knew, these men and women, what Raigmore had done. The first radio messages from Mars since its conquest had already come in. The Nwyllans were going. Most of them had already gone.

The point which Raigmore had found most difficult to

win in the end was not his own safety, but the safety of the Martian colonists. The Nwyllans understood and agreed that they would have to leave Mars, but automatically, inevitably, they would destroy everything there before leaving it. They were leaving the solar system meantime because Raigmore had convinced them that they couldn't conquer it. But naturally they would weaken it all they could in doing so.

Raigmore had to show the Nwyllans what the effect on the Terrans of slaughter such as they intended would be. He showed them what Hate was like. Since he could put the emotion direct into their minds, they were able to understand what humans motivated by a force so strong would be liable to do.

In the end they went, they surrendered, chiefly because they knew they were out of their depth. It wasn't surprising that Raigmore understood both them and the humans, but they had already found that the Martian colonists appeared to understand them better than they understood the colonists. Raigmore played on this. He wasn't surprised to find that the colonists had been subjected but not destroyed. The Nwyllan idea of Empire was a lot of races subject to Nwylla. There was no point in destroying their subjects, nor even in destroying a people they couldn't subject. They would leave such a people in the hope that sometime in the future they would be able to subject it. As they were leaving Earth.

It was as a conqueror that Raigmore returned. The mob below wasn't concerned with how he had done what he had done, only with the results. Raigmore had told them how to fight a battle, had fought the battle, and after it he had gone and spoken to the enemy and they had run away.

Raigmore knew that Alison wouldn't be there in the crowd about him. She would be waiting for him once he had run the gantlet of acclaim, but she wouldn't expose herself needlessly to the wild enthusiasm of the mob.

He opened the airlock of his ship, cautiously, and Alison was in his arms. She tried to stand straight and firm, yet he could feel in the contact of their bodies how afraid she had been.

Thousands of policemen and navy men held the crowd back as the man who had been a Nwyllan greeted his wife.

Gloria was left in charge at Washington. That was the lot of the Yellows; the Whites passed the reins back to them the first instant it was possible. There was a lot to do, but nothing, now, that Gloria and Morton and the new President, a man named Hewison, couldn't handle.

As the other four lay in the sun on a Californian beach, Alison remarked: "We're taking up where we left off the day Gloria came in and told us Robertson was murdered."

"Except Fred's here," said Margo. She was serenely happy now. She had discovered at last, with some surprise, that it was quite possible to like Salter better than Raigmore.

"Only partly here," came Salter's voice from underneath a huge sun hat. "Some of me is chasing the Nwyllans and making sure they don't come back. I haven't the supreme confidence in this sort of solution that you seem to have, Raigmore."

Raigmore was no longer in any position of authority. He would assume authority again automatically if the Nwyllans returned, but only then. He looked at Alison. She nodded, agreeing with Salter. She and Salter were relieved, but not elated. It wasn't their idea of victory, the purely human idea of victory. There were no treaties, no gains; the Nwyllans might be back at any moment, and always, from now on, Earth and Nwylla would know of each other and develop in natural opposition. Always there would be a struggle until one idea, backed by enormous force, overcame the other.

"What do you think, Margo?" he asked.

Margo shrugged her creamy shoulders that were still, Raigmore thought, her best point. "It's beyond me," she admitted. "Remember I'm only a Red Star."

"Beautiful but dumb," said Salter from under the hat. "In every two thousand people, there's only one thousand nine hundred ninety-nine stupider than you."

Margo smiled. "Anyway, doesn't the fact that the four of us are here together, with histories like ours, prove something?" she asked.

"It does," said Raigmore. "Listen, I'll tell you a little story. Once upon a time a flute and a bassoon sat next to each other in an orchestra. They didn't get on well at all. The flute kept cutting through all the bassoon's deep-voiced comments, and he didn't like it a bit. And as for the flute, whenever she had something particularly brilliant to say, there he was, making snide remarks at the bottom of his voice.

"But secretly they each wished they were more like the

other. And when they got home, the bassoon looked at his crooked windpipe and tried to straighten himself and sing higher. Meanwhile, on the other side of town, the flute was standing on tiptoe and trying to talk in a deep voice.

"They didn't go back until they'd practiced for a long time. Then at last they came in and sat down and turned haughtily to look at each other.

"And they were both clarinets."

Salter threw his sun hat, full of sand, at Raigmore. "And they made you a White Star," he moaned.

"Wait a minute," said Alison. "You don't really mean that, Eldin, do you?"

"That they were both clarinets?" demanded Salter derisively.

"Margo and I were only given human bodies," said Raigmore. "How much difference do you think that really makes? Are the emotions purely physical? I don't believe it. The Nwyllans have gone home to puzzle out what emotion can be. And some of us are gradually learning, Sally Morris tells me, to strip our concepts clean of emotion . . ."

He saw they weren't ready yet to see that Nwyllans and Terrans, now that the contact had been made, must gradually grow toward understanding. It didn't matter.

He put his hand on Alison's hot brown arm and caressed it gently.

"Oh well," he said. "Look at it another way if you like. I can't see competition as a bad thing. The Nwyllans will keep mankind together always, merely by existing. Nothing like that has ever happened to mankind before."

He closed his eyes against the glare of the sun. "I'm not

sorry," he went on, "but quite glad of the perpetual threat, the perpetual challenge, the perpetual need to put first things first. A race only fails when it no longer has anything worth doing. Don't the Nwyllans—strong, organized, different, with their vast Empire of different races in subjection—supply human beings, whenever they're ready, with something worth doing?"